I0738478

# TO BE PHOENIX

Cadillac Press

Cadillac Press
New Brunswick, Canada



2 4 6 8 10 9 7 5 3 1
FIRST EDITION THIS PUBLISHER

# NOVELS BY WENDY L. KOENIG

Sentient
Insurrection
One to Lose
Under Twin Suns
The Last Griffin
Birthright
Frozen Fire

OTHER BOOKS

Boo and Oscar in the Fantastic Fudge Fiasco
Le Gran Sault
Sunlit Night, Coffee and Sweet Dreams
Fear, Swallowed
Lions in the Closet
These Burning Stones

*Thank you to Debbie, Denise, Barb, Marcia, Lloyd, Larry, Vince, Eve, and Michelle. Your help has been invaluable!*

# TO BE PHOENIX

Wendy L. Koenig

CHAPTER 1

The flame of life licked throughout Destante's body. She shuddered, drawing in a breath, and opened her eyes to the inky well of a starless night. As always in those times, it had taken her awhile to get her bearings. To understand that she'd died. Again.

Her body remembered, though. Every cell of it ached, even as the burning hot blood of new vitality coursed through it, mending broken bones, cuts, and ruptured organs. She'd always thought it an odd sensation, this burning from the inside out, the undefined pressure, or a pinch deep inside her. Of course, she wouldn't be completely healed for a few more days yet. She'd have to be careful until then. She let her eyes close, concentrating on the changes within her. Trying to remember what had brought her to this point.

Judging by the aged smell of charred smoke in the air, she'd been burnt. That meant she'd been in the healing process a long time. Probably much longer than her usual few days.

As she became more aware of her surroundings, it slowly dawned on her she smelled very little of the harsh smoke from the volcano near her home. She'd been taken far to meet her attempted final death.

She also wasn't alone. There was an ink black shadow in the clearing with her, and it was moving.

She didn't want to disrupt any healing that might be going on in her spine; it would take her that much longer to become whole again. But, she also needed to know who was there, so she carefully turned her head toward the intruder and opened her eyes. Though it was dark, she could see quite well. After all, she had bird sight; she could see equally well, both night and day.

About fifteen feet away, she saw the image of a man in his early-thirties squatted on an oblong boulder that jutted a couple feet out of the ground. Really, though, how could she tell his age just by looking? She, herself, only looked to be in her late twenties, but was at that time nearly three hundred years old.

Judging by the height of his knees popped up in front of him, he was tall. He also had no paunch to push his legs away from his body. His shoulders were broad and his biceps looked well-muscled. She couldn't see the color of his hair, but she knew it was light brown, unlike her red. He wasn't solid like a real body should be; she could see right through him. A ghost, then.

Her father wasn't really there. Her injured mind also needed time to mend, to make the transition between death and life. Until it was whole again, it would play tricks with her, dredging up memories of past rebirths, making them seem like a current event. Confusing her or blanking out.

"Father," She said, her voice soft, barely stronger than a passing thought.

He cleared his throat and said, "Welcome back to

the living, little phoenix." It was something he'd always said, every time she'd died and been reborn. Then he slowly faded away.

He'd died shortly before she and her sister had moved many of the phoenix families here, to Mexico, near the turn of the tenth century, barely over 200 years ago. When all the dragons disappeared from the face of the Earth.

All but one. That one hid in the midst of the phoenixes.

CHAPTER 2

Elis, one of the kings of the griffin shapeshifters, slowly strolled around the man standing in front of the throne, looking him up and down. Elis, himself, was a tall man, broad and strong. He'd won many battles in the ongoing war with the dragons. He overshadowed the man before him in all ways.

The volcano, Colima, was busy tonight, filling the skies with foul smelling smoke. And the night was a dark and desperate one, storm clouds heavy overhead. The lanterns in the hall quivered with every breath of wind, sending shadows twisting grotesquely across the man's body. It was hard to get a read on him.

At last, Elis stopped in front of the man and asked, "Are you sure about the dragon shifter?"

He'd heard the rumor of an existing dragon. But he'd had no luck in finding out if the information was true. Then, this man had offered the truth. If there was even any trace of deception, he'd have the royal guard spear him through.

The man nodded. His voice held steady when he

answered. "I am."

"And what is it you seek in recompense?"

"Only that my people be spared and allowed to stay when your troops march across our lands."

"No title? Nothing but your people?" Angry pleasure filled Elis.

"That is all." A harsh gust billowed through the hall and the lanterns nearly went out. The man's face became a death mask.

"Very well, then. I will require two things of you. First, as plans are bandied about, and they will be, send word of them by courier at night. And second, send another courier immediately if something untoward happens."

"It shall be done to the best of my abilities."

CHAPTER 3

Destante stopped to wipe the sweat out of her eyes and looked up at the west coast Mexican sky. Except for the thick column of smoke from Colima, it was pale blue and right at midday. Perfect timing. The guards would be busy eating their noonday *almuerzo* of fish, beans, and tortillas.

It had been a week since her rebirth, and her memory was still foggy in parts; she didn't recognize the dim and musty place in front of her. It reeked of mold, mud, urine, and rotting food. It must be part of the villa, but which end? Did she turn left or right? Or backtrack completely? If only she could remember!

Spying a door in the back right corner, she crossed the open expanse.

Pinpricks raised the hairs on the back of her neck as something scraped across the packed earth floor behind her and a shadow raced across the open space toward her. She whirled to see a thick-set man on a giant, dark brown horse bearing down on her. A long, mean-looking sword hung from a scabbard on the saddle's side, and the rider's shaggy black hair swayed and bounced with every move of the horse.

She stepped out of his way, but the rider adjusted course immediately. With a start, she realized he meant to run her down.

Searching for a hiding place, she chose a pillar and dodged behind it just in time, the horse so close it brushed against her. The rider hauled on the reins to stop. The sound of the grunting horse as it turned, cat-like, filled the space to bursting. The horse dropped its haunches, whirled, and leapt toward her again.

She made a break toward the open yard.

Glancing behind her, she saw the rider bearing down on her again. He planted a booted foot in the middle of her back as he passed, knocking her to the ground, filling her mouth with blood.

He stopped, whirled again to face her, grinned, and backed his horse until he was standing between her and the way out. The only sound was the echo of the dark horse's billowing.

Destante scrambled to her feet, wiping grime on her skirt. "What do you want with me?"

The *guardia's* horse didn't move, nor did the rider answer. She knew now she was fighting for her life.

He drove the heels of his boots deep into his mount's sides and the huge animal lunged toward her, toes digging deep into the packed earth. Instead of running, she waited until he was almost upon her, then she ran straight at the horse, waving her arms and screaming. The creature swerved hard away from her with wild eyes and she grabbed the rider's leg, bracing herself.

Destante's arms were nearly ripped out of their sockets as the rider was jerked backward in his saddle.

She fell again, the salt of blood once more filling her mouth. The rider, however, managed to stay in his seat, leaning precariously to one side. When he reseated himself and whirled this time, a dark snarl framed his face.

He sat, waiting. Time stretched.

The giant horse fidgeted.

Destante changed tactics and lunged toward the recessed door. As the rider parried, moving his mount to block her, she dropped to the ground and rolled under the horse's belly.

One of the hooves grazed her cheek, sending tears and black spots to her eyes. Out the other side, she again bolted for the door, the rider cursing behind her as he tried to get his suddenly skittish mount under control.

Destante reached the door, wrestled it open, and darted inside.

Turning, she tugged the door shut behind her. The *guardia* would have to dismount to open it and she needed as much time as she could muster. She bolted up a short flight of red stone steps. At the top was a long hall, full of lamps and dusty paintings.

Memories sifted around her like burning dust. She and her sister walking that hall, tall and regal. Laughing, chasing her sister. Sneaking late at night to her lover's room. Years and centuries of memories.

Already, the rider had the entry wedged open, and the clatter of the horse's hooves filled the stairwell. To the right, the hall was long and devoid of doors until near the end. To the left, a nearby door stood wide open, letting sunlight spill into the hall. Destante bolted for the opening, the sound of the horse huffing up the steps adding speed to her panic.

She rounded the corner into the room, half blinded

by the light, only to find herself face to face with a
large knot of armed *guardias*.

# CHAPTER 4

From where he sat in the shadows, Aniause watched the commotion with hope. His heart surged within him. Destante had returned. After all this time. He'd thought she was gone for good.

She was different this time. Her hair was darker, nearly auburn. Her nose was also shorter, and her heart-shaped face a bit longer. She didn't quite look like herself, yet she did. It was her. His heart knew it.

Destante fought like a wild thing, swinging and kicking at the *guardias* who held her. Her clothes were grungy and the soles of her shoes were worn and thin. Yet, she had to be an answer to Pirien's prayers. Why else would she have shown up at this auspicious hour?

Just that morning he and the priest had been discussing their problem.

Pirien had stood in the center of Aniause's laboratory, trying not to touch anything, for fear of dirtying his official robes. He looked disdainfully at the overburdened tables and dusty alchemist tools. "You know Baldric will turn over the dragon to Elis in exchange for the safety of his people."

"I know. He may be the rightful heir, but there has to be something we can do." Aniause circled the room. He kept his hands busy, straightening towers of envelopes that contained powders for his medicinal drinks and salves. His mind whirled through all the possibilities.

"I've been praying f—"

Aniause scoffed. "Prayer! What good does that do?"

Pirien was quiet a moment, watching Aniause work. He straightened the folds in his robe and softly asked, "There's nothing you can do?"

"He doesn't listen to me, or else I would have done it." He stopped and met his ancient friend's gaze, taking a deep breath and letting it out slowly. "Well, there's nothing else to it, then. Baldric will become our king. We'll just have to limit as much of his damage as we can."

Now, in the moments before the crowning, Destante suddenly burst upon them, as if a gift from above.

## CHAPTER 5

Destante struggled with the contingent of *guardias*.
Behind her, the sound of the horse's hooves came closer
in the hallway, bringing her tormentor to her. A gust of
fresh air from the wide open balconied window taunted
her with freedom. If she could just get loose from the
multitude of hands....

Two robed men stood between her and that
window. The man on the left was ancient: stoop-
shouldered and grey-haired. He had a puzzled
expression on his wrinkled face. Names and faces
floated through her mind, but none matched.

Then it came to her, like a dove on the summer
breeze. The man's name was Pirien. In his hands, he
held a bible. He was the priest. He was important. On
the table beside him sat a purple pillow with gold trim.
On the pillow: a crown. A coronation? What had
happened to her sister? Who was being crowned?

After a moment of frowning, the identity of the
man on the right came to her: her cousin, Baldric. He

would be the intended king. By contrast to Pirien, his hair was dark brown and his face had far fewer lines. He snarled, "What is the meaning of this?!?"

The bulk of the rider entered on foot behind her and bowed low.

"Javier. I might have known! Take your sport elsewhere!"

Javier stood and snatched her hair, wrenching her from the *guardias* who held her. She tried to swing at him, but her fists made no contact.

At that moment, a third man stepped out from the shadows behind the bookcases at the right of the room. His robe was dark blue and he had no wrinkles, other than those at the corners of his black eyes. His long, thin mustache matched the light brown of his hair. Stopping in front of her, his gaze inspected every inch of her body, finally settling on her face. His eyes were soft, as was his smile.

This was a man she knew well. This was Aniause. He was the only reason she'd come home. Her heart stilled and she felt her face flush with the heat of love. She smiled back.

Behind him, her cousin snapped, "Javier!"

The grey-haired Pirien held up his hand, belaying the order. To Aniause, he asked, "What do you see?"

Aniause spun her around and tugged down her sleeve to expose the royal mark on her shoulder. Immediately, he knelt in front of her. "Princess Destante!"

There was a long moment of silence. Baldric paled. Then he said, "Destante!?! It cannot be! She's dead!"

"You're certain, Aniause?" the elderly Pirien gently asked.

Aniause rose and nodded. Turning to a thick man in a ranking guards uniform, he said, "Uzdal, fetch her most recent painting. There should be one on the wall in the dining hall."

As he hurried away, Baldric paled even more, his brow creasing in silent fury.

Pirien rubbed his finger across the mark on her shoulder, "This mark is quite old. Which it should be, even though she regenerated. She's the right age, but she looks very different. More than usual."

Destante frowned. Why had Aniause revealed her identity? She didn't want this and he knew it. They'd spent many many years together as lovers. He knew her better than anyone. She'd told him many times she'd never take the throne. She hadn't come back for that. She'd come back for him. To ask him to join her far away from this place.

Aniause focused on her again, nodding slowly, thoughtfully. "Pirien, I believe it IS her."

She opened her mouth to beg forgiveness for interrupting their ceremony, to explain she wasn't the person they thought she was, but his gaze caught hers and held it. An understanding passed between them. She snapped her mouth shut.

Baldric said, "It can't be. This is an imposter. Destante's dead, I tell you."

"You saw to that, did you?" Pirien said dryly, disdain plain across his withered face as he glanced at her cousin.

He stopped, confused. "I gave orders ..."

Aniause turned carefully to Baldric. "Obviously, you failed to prevent the rebirth process."

The chief guard, Uzdal, reappeared with a huge painting and stood it beside her. The woman pictured there had long golden-red hair, large lips, and a heart-shaped face. Not quite like Destante was now, but the resemblance was unmistakable.

Pirien knelt. "Princess!"

As the others in the room knelt, Baldric whispered, "No!" He snapped his gaze back and forth from her to the painting. Slowly, his mouth open in disbelief, he dropped to his knees and bowed his head.

CHAPTER 6

Destante stood in center of the marbled room beside Aniause, facing those bowed before her. She could tell everyone a lie: that she wasn't really the Queen's sister. She might be killed if they believed her, though. Or at the very least, given back to Javier.

She should tell Aniause, though. He, of all people, would know how she felt. He could sort out this problem. She whispered, "I don't want to be Queen."

He nodded very slowly, turning his back on Baldric. When he spoke, it was a whisper. "I know. But, we need you. Your sister is gone. Our kingdom is in on the brink of battle, and you're a better choice than your cousin. Like it or not, you need to take your place on the throne. We can discuss this further later, if you wish."

It seemed, for now, that she was to be Queen. For centuries, she'd avoided the throne, leaving it to her sister instead. Now time had caught up with her.

Baldric fumed in the shadows of the room, then pivoted on his heel and marched toward the door, his boot heels hard on the marble. Uzdal stepped in his way with even black eyes, as if daring him to try to pass. A pair of guards gripped the lord's arms.

Uzdal said, "For the crime of attempted assassination, you will be imprisoned until the queen can deal with you as she sees fit."

As they led Baldric away, Aniause turned her to face Pirien, who began a litany. Those in the room rose to their feet in silence. Some were in their traditional European clothing, some in formal Mexican bright colors and gold trim. Many were phoenix lords, but there were also shifter royals from other species present: wolves, bears, various birds, and more. The room was full to capacity, though the griffins were conspicuously absent.

As the priest droned on, what felt like a spark ignited deep within her. It fanned white hot, and then turned to a small flickering flame. The royal fire, passed through the royal line to the ruling phoenix. In olden days there were many rulers, many flames. Now, there was only her. Those under her care were the last of the phoenixes.

When her sister had assumed the crown, she'd tried to describe this flickering spark to Destante, but there had been no adequate words.

The heat was unbearable. Her hands and arms were bright red, and she imagined her face was also. Probably all of her. She wanted to loosen her clothes, or strip naked and dive into the nearby ocean. Sweat slid down her calves to puddle in her shoes.

Then Pirien was done, and Destante hadn't heard a thing he'd said, so focused on the fire which now lived within her.

Aniause leaned forward and whispered, "Kneel."

When she did, Pirien placed the crown on her head.

The cool metal ring bit into her scalp as did the weight of the responsibility. Though the crown was not worn except in formal functions, the duties were just as heavy as they'd always been.

Aniause took her hand, lifting her. He turned her to the crowd in the room and, in a strong voice, he said, "Behold, the Queen of the phoenixes."

She smiled at those who represented her people, human and phoenix alike, as they applauded, some politely, some with exuberance.

The heat raged within her.

Aniause nodded at Javier, who approached and immediately kneeled.

"My Queen, this man tried to cause you harm. He is deserving of punishment." He turned his back to Javier and whispered, "He's a good fellow, just overzealous in his duties."

She took a deep breath. She was now the queen, at least until her sister was found. She wondered, idly, if there would be two phoenixes with flames at that point.

Focusing on her task, she realized she had no idea what to do with the errant guard. "Javier, you are deserving of punishment and will receive it once I've had time to reflect."

Destante nodded to two of the *guardias* and they bodily lifted Javier to his feet, escorting him out of the room.

She turned to Aniause. "We need to speak. I don't want this."

"I know. We'll talk later. But there's a banquet now. First, though, I need to treat your injury. Is this the only place?" He touched the place on her cheek where the horse's hoof had grazed her.

She nodded and blushed. His touch had left a tingling trail behind it, stirring the emotions she felt for him, eclipsing the phoenix flame.

At his request, a servant fetched a stringent ointment from his lab. Aniause moved in close and dabbed the medicine on her cheek.

His natural musk sent her heart into chaotic lunges against her ribs. She loved him with everything within her. She'd come back for him. For love.

When he'd finished doctoring her, he led her to the great dining hall where her guests waited. The long table was overburdened with trays and bowls of every food type. Servants stood at the edge of the room, ready to jump at the smallest request.

As they walked to her place at the head of the table, she leaned close to Aniause and whispered, "You're not to leave me until everything is over."

"Yes, My Queen."

"Stop calling me that!"

Aniause didn't respond. He smiled, though, as he settled her into her seat.

Throughout the afternoon and into the evening, Destante allowed her hand to be kissed by a multitude of people. She heard dozens of toasts and received scores of gifts. Many people didn't try to hide their surprise, nor their disgust at her sudden appearance and ruination of Baldric's plans.

Aniause often cast long glances at her, watching with a grim smile and dark, piercing eyes.

At last the night was over, and she was escorted to her room. A stiff guard stood silently at the door.

Aniause bowed and kissed her hand. "I see you're tired. We'll speak tomorrow, My Queen. Ask for me when you're ready. A *sirvienta* has been appointed to see to your needs. Sleep well." Then, he whisked away before she could even whisper his name.

With regret, she watched him go. He was right, of

course. Aniause was nearly always right. She was tired and needed sleep. Still, she wished he would have stayed, as he had in the past. But, she was queen now. How much would change because of that small detail?

Inside, a young native girl waited with night clothes in hand. Silently, she helped Destante change and then left.

Throwing herself on the bed, the queen of the phoenixes let sleep take her.

CHAPTER 7

Javier was miserable. True, his *cárcel* was nothing
more than a locked, guarded room. Not at all like Elis's
dark dungeon with mold, rats, and lice. Sadly, he'd
experienced that one first hand. Here, he was sitting on
a clean, straw-filled mattress, leaning against a dry
wall. He could grow to be comfortable there.

No, he was miserable because he'd made a mess of
things again. It seemed to be his pattern. He was good
at his job and had always been promoted through the
ranks quickly, no matter where he was. But then things
always got difficult.

In Elis's case, one of the king's mistresses had
noticed him, once he'd made the rank of *capitán*. Her
smile had been his undoing and Elis had caught them
together in her bed chambers. Javier had sat in that
dungeon for months. But, even though *el cárcel* had
been dismal, he'd had company.

Eventually, when it had become overcrowded, he'd
been released and had come here. Where he'd tried to
run down *la reina*. She'd looked like a peasant, not

royalty. How was he to know? She should have announced herself. That's what royalty did, wasn't it?

He shook his head at his bad luck and stared at the corner where the ceiling met the wall across from him. Escape was always a possibility. He'd done it other places.

Between the *guardias* staring at the door and the solid walls, he doubted he could escape alone. The traitor, Baldric, was in a cell near his, but he refused to speak, though Javier had whispered near the wall many times. There would be no help escaping.

His crime had to be akin to Baldric's attempted assassination. It seemed *la muerte* had finally found him.

## CHAPTER 8

Aniause sat alone in the dark. He was in Pirien's room, because all he'd done since leaving the queen was pace and fuss with his laboratory equipment and ancient texts. Destante was back. Not only back, but was now on the throne. She was royalty. And he had common blood.

The thought tortured him. He wanted to go to her bed, to be with her. He'd been a year without her and that was far too long. Phoenixes mated for the duration of all their lives, throughout all their rebirths. The grief within him, borne from the belief she was permanently dead, needed to be soothed away. His pain tortured him. So, he'd abandoned the torment of his own rooms. He needed quiet and space and, right now, that was in the priest's chambers.

Also, misery loved company.

Naturally, Pirien wasn't in.

Aniause let himself into the priest's room and settled into a deep walnut chair. The griffins were threatening them. And like it or not, Destante was exactly the person they needed on the throne. She had a cool keen mind that was quick and sure. But something had been bothering him since the griffin's plans had become apparent. Who had told them there was a dragon still alive? Told them that the dragon resided in the very heart of the phoenixes? Bribes had been paid to keep everyone quiet. Then, Destante had been killed, followed quickly by her sister, allowing Baldric to assume the throne. He was the obvious choice, but did he work alone?

Strumming his fingers on the arm of his usurped chair, Aniause was just thinking of leaving when his ancient friend arrived, tankard of pulque, the local fermented drink, in hand.

The priest paused at the door. Steadied himself on the frame as the ground beneath them shivered. "The volcano has been busy lately."

Aniause gripped the arms of the chair, waiting out the quake. It didn't last long, merely a subtle reminder of the power contained in the earth.

As the tremor subsided, Pirien entered, shutting the door behind him and placing the liquor on the nearby table. "I thought you'd be here, Aniause. I see you've made yourself comfortable."

He slid his white robe off his shoulders, deftly catching it before it hit the floor. He folded it and placed it in his deeply-grained imported walnut wardrobe. Of all the rooms in the villa, including the queen's, this one was the most lavish, with heavy religious tapestries lining every wall, the rich walnut furniture, and thick white bedding. Gold adorned every trapping and turn.

"Congratulations are in order." Reaching into a small cabinet, Pirien pulled out two silver goblets and filled them with the thick, white alcohol. He held out a goblet.

Aniause waved the drink away. If there was anything to lift his gloom, it wasn't pulque. He slowly said, "It came at a high enough cost."

The old priest looked thoughtfully at Aniause. After a moment, he shrugged and said, "We had to stop Baldric's plan. You know that. Do you think she can do it?"

Aniause slowly nodded. "We can teach her what she doesn't know."

Pirien sank into the second walnut chair and took a long drink. "There's a lot for her to learn. Furthermore, we won't be able to leave her alone for even a minute. Her death, and that of her sister, suggests the assassins won't stop."

Aniause rubbed his forehead. That's what he'd feared, why he was stewing. "It's a dual pronged dilemma. You and I cannot be with her every second, even if we neglect our duties. And we can't let my past with her cloud the public's perception of her. We need another person, but for the life of me, I can't think of anyone we can trust. Not even our *guardias*."

They sat silent a moment, Pirien sipping from his goblet and Aniause staring blankly at a tapestry of St. George. Then the ancient priest cleared his throat. "How about Javier? She needs a personal guard assigned to her and I believe he'd do anything to get back into good standing, including working with us."

Aniause turned his head and stared at his old friend. "You're a genius."

He stood and helped himself to the liquor. Tomorrow he'd speak to Baldric. Tonight, he'd let the thick liquid burn his worries away.

CHAPTER 9

"Javier is in Jail?" Elis snorted. Leave it to his ex-captain to make a mess of things. It was late night, but through the tall window of the great hall, there was a smoky glow over the dome of Colima. The volcano had shaken the ground twice that day, once within the last hour. His city was safe from any violence the volcano might flow down on them, but the quakes destroyed his buildings. His castle had even recently developed several cracks what would need attending soon.

"Yes, Sire. It seems he tried to run down the new queen." The courier, sent from one of the phoenix lords, shifted his weight, his eyes following every move his master made.

"Hah! I suppose I shouldn't be surprised. It seemed inevitable." Elis shook his head, recalling when Javier had landed in his own cells. Trust was earned; Javier had earned it quickly, and then betrayed it. He sighed at the lost plans he'd made for that young captain. But Javier wasn't the important news.

He said, more to himself than to the man standing in front of him. "So, Destante has returned and has taken the throne from Baldric. He must be consumed with anger. The question is, will she follow her cousin's counsel or walk in her late sister's footsteps?"

He glanced at the courier not expecting an answer, but as a way of shifting his thoughts. The man looked at him quizzically, but Elis didn't explain; his thoughts were already moving on. There was a third option: the new queen could pack up her kingdom and leave. But he would find them. There was nowhere she and that dragon could go that they wouldn't be found.

The fourth option, that she would stay and fight, was just too ludicrous. Only a fool would stand and face his massive army. Still, greater follies had been committed through the course of this thousand year war.

Elis cleared his throat and said to the courier, "You may return to your station. Send word to Noll about the queen's appearance. Keep me apprised of any new developments."

The courier gave one single nod which turned into a half-bow and departed with quick jerky strides.

Elis stared out the window at the volcano glow, deep in his thoughts. For now, he would do nothing. Let the new queen commit to her decision, and then he would destroy her anyway.

## CHAPTER 10

Though exhausted, that night Destante dreamed an old familiar dream. One that was actually a recent memory from nearly two hundred years ago, when her family still lived in Spain. Long before they'd moved to this new country where the thousand-year shapeshifter war had been quiet lately.

It was a bright day. Battle was all around. Her father and sister were in the sky, tearing at the enemy with claw and beak. Her father was one of the last fire-bearers left alive, burning all who came too near. Destante and Aniause had elected to skim low over the ground, searching the ground for any enemy foot soldiers foolish enough to traverse the green, open fields. They also dispatched the fallen injured. The phoenixes would be reborn, and the enemy would go to whatever afterlife awaited them. Any allies that were found injured were sent to Aniause's hospital for treatment upon his return.

She'd just finished a run, when she heard a thick roar from above. Turning her attention to the clouds, she saw her father, flames bright, speeding toward a line of griffins. As he neared, the closest griffin peeled out of line to escape the heat of the fire, allowing the griffin behind to get closer to the king of phoenixes.

Belatedly, Destante realized she'd allowed herself to stay too close to the ground. As she moved to regain her height, a long slim point of a spear drove deep into her chest, dropping her to the floor of the meadow, dying.

The last things she saw were her father being decapitated in the clouds, his head carried off far from his body so he couldn't be reborn, and Aniause destroying the man who'd killed her.

Destante woke, her head aching and her neck sore from the weight of the crown all the evening before. With a groan, she rolled over and stared at the broken bits of light that shone long across the floor from deeply chiseled windows. Fractured light like her fractured life.

And now she was the queen of the phoenixes, with fire burning inside her. Of course, the world saw her as nothing more than a wealthy land owner, with many tenants and employees working her property.

How did this happen to her? It was the last thing she wanted.

Tiny feet shuffled into her field of vision and a soft Mexican-accented voice said, "Good Morning, Ma'am. *El doctor* requests to be sent for when you're ready."

*El doctor?* Did she mean Aniause? Another memory pushed forward: The overwhelming gulf of loneliness while he was abroad studying medicine.

"I've prepared *un baño* for you." The *sirvienta's* bare feet hurried away, but returned in a moment. "Ma'am?"

An anxious, sharp-chinned face lowered into view

and dark eyes with dark lashes peered at Destante. She now saw that it was the same maid from the night before.

The girl asked, "Are you ill? Should I send for *el doctor* now?" The feet scurried for the door.

With that, Destante struggled upright, wincing at the sharp screams of pain from her neck and shoulder muscles. "No!"

The girl stopped, mouth open as if in mid-sentence. Then she hurried back.

Destante blinked. Gods, the girl was fast! "You said you prepared a bath?"

"*Sí. Un baño.*" Again the curtsy. She led the way to an adjacent room with walls covered in multi-colored tiles. On a raised platform in the center of the room was a sunken pool with a large phoenix design in the tile on the bottom. Steam rose from the water and rose petals floated on the surface sending soft fragrances into the air.

Destante had never seen anything so beautiful. Her sister had never allowed her in there.

The girl lowered her gaze. "I wanted it *especial* for you."

"What's your name? And how old are you?"

"Adelita." At that, the girl curtsied once more. "I'm fourteen."

"Where are you from?" Destante shed her night clothes, letting them fall to the floor.

"I am first from east of Tula. But my parents moved here with my *tío* Roberto a few years ago."

Destante stepped down into the water. A shiver of delight spread across her as the scented warmth surrounded her. She relaxed against the edge of the pool and Adelita poured water down the back of her hair.

Though the girl had been quiet the night before, it

seemed the questions had opened the floodgate; the girl kept up a constant chatter during the course of the bath and, by the time it was over and Destante was dressed in bright Mexican finery, Adelita had divulged every detail of her life thus far.

"I'll send for *el doctor* now." Adelita curtsied and scurried away.

Destante raced after her, narrowly beating her to the door. She smiled at her startled *sirvienta*. "I'll go to him."

She escaped out the door and into blessed silence.

# CHAPTER 11

It took Destante a bit of time to find Aniause's laboratory. Her memory was still playing tricks on her. Though the villa wasn't huge, she turned down a wrong passage that she was positive was a connecting hallway. Coming back, she got turned around and found herself in the kitchen. The staff froze in their tasks, all watching her with wide eyes.

She took a deep breath, closed her eyes, and focused on the villa's layout in her mind. Then she smiled at the kitchen staff and set out to follow the path she'd decided upon.

Finally, she pushed open the heavy wooden door to Aniause's lab and grinned to herself. Thick tables were covered with odd clutter, strange gadgets, medical texts, vials of medicine, and bubbling samples. Dust hung in long slices of light let in by the tall thin windows. The table lamps sat atop everything in haphazard balance. It comforted her that he hadn't changed during her absence.

She picked up the closest book, a thick black tome with red lettering and read the spine aloud. "Leechbook of Bald."

From behind her, Aniause said, "It's quite good. It combines all aspects of Anglo-Saxon, Celtic, Greco-Roman, and Arab herbalism."

Startled, she whirled, bumping the corner of the desk and dropping the book to the floor. Her gaze roved over him. He looked good in typical Mexican white linen. His eyes twinkled pure pleasure at her. And that smile sent a deep sigh into her soul, curling a thrill into her stomach as it always had. They were two halves of the same whole. Unspoken mates forever.

They stared into each other's eyes a moment. She smiled, then bent and retrieved the book, handing it to him. He took it, his fingers lingering against hers. Abruptly he pulled away with a frown.

"I will come to you from now on, My Queen. It's not a good idea for you to be here." He returned the book to the desk, shoving aside the various trappings there, and stepped back, putting several strides between them.

But of course, she was now the queen.

He looked her up and down. "Your differences are more drastic this time. Your hair is darker. Your eyes are bluer. There are other differences, too."

"How long was I gone?"

From the safety of the middle of the room, he said, "Long enough. Over a year."

"My body was burnt. It took time to regenerate."

"The irony of burning a phoenix. " He cracked a lopsided smile at that and her breath caught at the simple gesture. How many times had she seen that? Kissed those lips?

He continued, "Baldric claims he 'saw to it'

himself, but I wonder. Did you see him?"

She shook her head, shaking the longing away. "I didn't see anyone. Three of them came at me in the dark from behind. I was unconscious from then on."

"Shame. It would have been nice to have caught Baldric in the act this time."

"Where's my sister?"

His face softened and he spoke gently. "I suspect he succeeded with her. Though, again, we have no proof he was involved at all. He's clever."

She nodded. First get rid of the sister, then the queen herself. As the next in the bloodline, it made her cousin the ruler. The coronation ceremony she'd interrupted meant her sister had died over a fortnight ago. "You don't know, though?"

"We've been unable to find the body. However, because you didn't return after the required fortnight waiting period, we assumed you were permanently gone as well." He shook his head, his eyes darkening beyond black, into tiny wells devoid of light. "Nearly killed me."

After a moment, he shook his head and continued, "Baldric might have thought he succeeded with your death and so killed your sister the same way. It will take time for us to know for certain if she'll return or not."

"So, until then, I'm queen. Just great." She scowled and stared out the window. A thick fog that had rolled in from the ocean overnight was being burned off by the sun. Another hot day.

Aniause followed her. Stood right beside her. The heat of his body burned into her memories of close nights with nothing between them but skin.

He said, "We believe your life is still in danger. Baldric is bound to try again, even from his jail cell. We don't know who we can trust."

He hesitated and then asked, "Do you remember that guardsman you threw in prison yesterday?"

She rolled her eyes. "Javier. I'm not likely to forget him."

"Appoint him as your personal guard. I think he'll be loyal."

She couldn't believe what she'd just heard. "He tried to run me down! Trust isn't the word I'd use regarding him."

"He was acting out of loyalty to the throne. Albeit, a little overzealously. He's a better bet than most of the rest of your men. I have no doubt he'll do anything to get back in your good graces. A man like that will stay loyal to the one who saves him from his own stupidity."

She shrugged. "Fine. But, Aniause, I won't tolerate being queen forever. I only came back to see you. I meant to sneak in, but Javier spoiled it."

He nodded, an uncomfortable cloud darkening his face. He spoke softly. "I would have given anything to find your body. To bring you home again."

She turned to him, but he took a step back, holding up his hands, warning her off. Those same hands used to hold her in the closest of embraces. "You are now queen. I'm just a doctor with no royal blood. Like it or not, there's a law against you and I being together. Your sister may never come back and there are shapeshifters all around us who will use any excuse to see you fall. I will not be the reason for dethroning you."

"Everyone knows we're life mates. We can't change that. But, we can keep it private, if you feel the need."

He shook his head, heartbreak clear in his eyes. "That's never worked well before. I see no reason for it to be any different now. What we had before can no longer exist."

CHAPTER 12

Aniause watched resignation settle over Destante's fine features. He'd give anything to see that smile again, to be the light in her eyes. But he was right and she knew it. He said, "I'm sorry. I know this is hard. It's nearly killing me too. But I firmly believe it's for the best that we obey the laws handed down from past generations. There's a reason they were put in place."

Anger seemed to flood over her like a tidal wave. Her face flushed and her eyes flashed. Her voice, though not raised, turned hard. "Laws from people so long ago that they have no bearing on today. Laws that should have been repealed by my sister years ago. Laws that everyone has always circumvented, including us. Except now you suddenly want to uphold this one single archaic monstrosity."

He sighed. "Your people are frightened. Even Baldric, though he'll never say it. We need you. We need the stability of knowing the phoenixes will always continue. The inheritance of the fire only passes through royal blood, you know this. You need to marry someone your own rank. Someone who can ensure future protection for the dragon."

Before she could come back with a quick retort, he raised his hand, cutting her off. "You know I'm right. It's why we never married, never had children, never even spoke of our bonding to anyone. And it's why you're so hurt and so angry. Because you know what's at stake."

Stained light from the windows cast shadows across her, cutting her angry frown into a horror mask. Her breaths were harsh, echoing furiously from the walls of the small room.

He squared his shoulders, taking on his sorrow as a thick blanket to hide within. "I sent for Javier to be brought to the hacienda where your breakfast awaits. I'll escort you."

"I believe I know where it is." She whirled, anger still clear on her face, the skirt of her dress flaring wide, and stormed from the lab.

Aniause followed, his hands clasped behind his back and his head lowered to keep from watching Destante's hips sway. Even the few moments together had gone a long way toward balming his wounded heart. And now, he wanted nothing more than to pull her to his private bedchamber, plead his apology, and share a passionate moment as they had many times in the past. Scolding himself, he shook his head sadly. Staying away from the woman he'd always loved was going to be a severe trial.

## CHAPTER 13

Destante settled into her chair at the outdoor table on the hacienda, always her favorite place. In the villa, guests who'd come for the coronation were packing, preparing to leave, their voices calling out to one another.  But here, she was distant from them, as if in another world. And right now she needed that distance, after what Aniause had decided. How would she make him change his mind? Could she? Was their bond strong enough to weather this?

Aniause joined her, seating himself, not beside her as he used to, but back from the table and to her right. For well over a hundred years, the two of them had eaten breakfast together after a long night of love making. But no more. As the cook brought her food, she sat back in her chair and sadly gazed at the scenery she'd always loved.

Most of her people had brought their European ways with them when they first immigrated from Spain over two centuries ago, in the year 811 AD. They built lavish castles, complete with knights and heralds. She and her sister had stones torn from the very mountain that held her now and had used them to build the villa. They'd embraced the Mexican culture.

The war was started by the death of a dragon shapeshifter prince at the hands of a witch and a griffin shifter. It had consumed the whole of the shifter world ever since. It was said it would continue until one side or the other was obliterated. Neither side knew the meaning of forgiveness, it seemed.

On the opposite side of the hacienda, down a sheer cliff and across a wide and sandy public beach was the might of the Pacific Ocean, pounding waves and pulsing with life. It's cool salt air flowed up to her, promising something, but what?

To her left was the town of Manzanillo, fast growing into a city. She couldn't see it because of the jut of mountain between them, but she knew it was there, as living as the sea. At night, some of the harbor boats went out into the ocean, their lights like pollen from a flower.

To her right, equally out of sight and quite some distance away, was the village of San Patricio.

And nearly straight behind her, up the steep slope on the other side of the villa, over the ridge and in griffin territory, were the two volcanoes, the taller Nevado de Colima and the more violent one known simply as Colima. This last, its true name Volcán de Fuego, often erupted, thundering ash and rock into the sky, blanketing the towns, the trees, and the villa. The recent quakes had been because of Colima. A thick, restless, black snake of smoke raised its head above the volcano. Time would tell whether it's threat would die away or escalate into an explosion.

It had always been this way. It always would be.

Like the ocean, it was unending.

Like a phoenix. As old as time itself.

As old as the final dragon shapeshifter that was now under her family's protection. There were so few phoenixes left, it seemed fitting the last dragon should hide in their midst.

Her army chief, Uzdal, and two Mexican *guardias* with long wicked machetes approached from the low buildings on the left, Javier between them, his arms tied behind his back. Though his walk was confident as he was brought across the yard, Destante read the insecurity in his gaze. The men stopped a few feet from the table and waited silently.

She took a sip of milky white tea and glanced at Aniause through the steam. His eyes were narrowed, watching her. Their gazes met and he nodded. With a sigh, she set down her cup and focused her attention on the two men who'd escorted Javier.

"Thank you. You may wait over there." She waved her hand toward the edge of the hacienda.

Without a word, the two *guardias* returned the way they'd come, long machetes slung low over their backs.

Uzdal said, "Your council is still here. They are waiting for you in the library."

Destante nodded. "They'll wait until I'm done here, I'm sure."

She scrutinized Javier with narrowed eyes. "Aniause seems to think I can trust you, that your attempt to injure or kill me was just an overzealous effort to do your job. Tell me, is this true?"

His eyes widened. He glanced at the doctor, then slid his gaze back to her. "*Sí.* I mean, yes Ma'am."

"What makes you trustworthy?"

"I want nothing more than to do *el trabajo*, my job, to the best of my abilities."

"Do you think doing your job includes trying to kill someone before anything can be learned about that person?"

His dark eyes blazed with anger. "You were trying to sneak into the villa, possibly to do harm to the next king. You'd already managed to bypass all the other *guardias*. Therefore, you were not to be treated easily because you might escape. Which you were trying to do. Yes, I think force was *justificado*." He stared at her, chest heaving with the passion of his beliefs.

Aniause spoke up. "Don't you think it would be better to bring your captive to us uninjured? She had no weapon."

"Just because I couldn't see one didn't mean she didn't have one. Some *armas* are easily *oculto*…hidden."

Destante cleared her throat. "There are ways to subdue people without injuring them."

His gaze fell. His shoulders slumped.

She nodded. Javier was smart and a fast thinker. And all appearances pointed to him having learned a lesson. He deserved a chance to redeem himself. But, he would bear close watching.

Beckoning Uzdal, she said, "Give him back his sword and untie him. I have a job for him."

Javier looked up at her surprised.

She dismissed Uzdal and the other guards and said, "Javier, I need a bodyguard. Someone who can quickly assess a threat and stop that person at all costs, no matter who it is. But you'd also need to be responsible enough to understand we need to question the attacker. Is that something you can do?"

"*Sí*. Yes, Ma'am." He nodded, eager and sincere.

From a side door in the villa, came Uzdal and the two *guardias* with Baldric. Out of deference to his ranking, her army chief had left the phoenix lord untied.

Destante gave a short bark of laughter and softly said, "Speak of the Devil."

Aniause smiled at that and Javier moved nearer to her, his fists clenched, muscles bunched.

Baldric strode quickly across the green, ignoring his escorts. As they neared, Baldric eyed Javier's stance. "My Queen, there is an urgent matter of state that requires your attention."

"And that would be?"

Baldric startled, faltering in his stride. He jerked his eyes from Javier to Aniause. "Er, it's a state matter."

"Speak."

"The griffins, Noll, to the north, and his cousin, Elis, to the east, are forming plans to attack us. I don't need to remind you how dangerous they are."

Aniause said, "That won't last. Those two have been fighting each other since the day they were born."

Baldric fixed an icy stare on the physician. "Only a fool would ignore the possible danger."

Aniause slowly stood, fire in his eyes. Then he hesitated, turned to Destante and bowed. "I will take my leave now, My Queen."

"I'll come find you when I am free again."

He nodded and left.

"Baldric, you may be my cousin, but if you wish to stay on my good side, you'll guard your tongue and show respect where it's due."

With a look of disbelief on his face, he gestured to where Aniause had been sitting. "He has no royal blood."

"I'm not arguing with you. And it's not a suggestion."

He clenched his jaw, once, twice. Then he bowed and said in a tight, low voice, "Yes, My Queen."

"Furthermore, there is the question of your attempted assassination."

His face reddened further, yet he said nothing.

She smiled at his discomfort. "Your exact words: I gave orders. Tell me what orders did you give? Finish the sentence you began."

He dropped to one knee. "I only seek to serve the royal throne."

Destante sighed. Baldric was far too clever to be caught this way. She'd have to wait until a more candid time to get the truth out of him. With a nod to Uzdal, she ordered his release.

CHAPTER 14

The volume in the library was such that Destante could hear the conversation before she even reached the second floor of the wide marble staircase. Strident voices warred with each other to be heard. Strangely, the words mostly had to do with her, rather than the upcoming threat of treaty.

"...from nowhere."

"Aniause stood against him."

"…looks like she has that guard with her."

The moment she entered the room, all conversation ceased. As Javier and Uzdal settled against the wall behind her, she took her seat at her desk. Baldric wound his way around the room to an empty chair. "Gentlemen, I'm happy that I'm so important and you're so free in your worries that you gossip about my well being. However, we have business to discuss." She was pleased to note that several faces turned a deep red.

Torag, a short balding man who was not a shapeshifter, but whose ancestors traveled from Spain with Destante's and Baldric's fathers, was seated near the center of the room. His great grandfather had originally been a man servant, but had been released upon arrival in Mexico. He'd done well in the centuries since, gaining many holdings. The distress on the lord's face was clear. "There is a rumor that the griffins have discovered we have the last dragon in our care. The whole shapeshifter world is in an uproar. Skirmishes are breaking out everywhere."

Baldric's twin brother, Balteus, spoke up from the crowd in the back of the room. "Elis and Noll are threatening to join forces. We've been told they intend to attack us. We could defeat one of them. Two, and they will crush our skulls like eggs."

Destante stood and went to the window. Steel colored clouds scudded across the sky until they merged with the ocean at the horizon. Tiny white dots that were pelicans floated across the reflected darker grey of the choppy water. "Exactly how many men do we have?"

"You have a little over forty." It was Baldric who answered this time.

"Why so few?" What had happened to her sister's army?

"The people refuse to fight. There is no money to pay." Baldric again.

She turned toward the room in astonishment. "There's no money? Where has it gone?"

The men looked at each other in uncomfortable silence. She knew the answer: her sister, Delcinae, had spread the money widely, bribing to silence those who knew about the dragon in their midst. But, her effort had apparently failed. Was there no loyalty in the soldiers?

Destante frowned and turned back to the window.

Near the coast, a fleet of fishing boats made a beeline toward Manzanillo. She choked back a laugh. They probably had more money than her kingdom did. It amazed her and she found herself shaking her head. The banquet last night must have cost a pretty penny. Baldric's money, no doubt. That thought brought out a wry grin.

The room behind her rustled uncomfortably. Voices murmured. Baldric's strident voice rose above. "This is not the time for indecision. We must act quickly to seek our own alliance with one or the other of them. As your sister did."

"'As my sister did.' You propose I bed one of them?" She refused to give the room the dignity of her facing them.

"That is a decision for you to consider, if you value your kingdom."

"I'll be no whore."

"It may be the only way to save us. As your sister found."

"Really. And which one would you suggest?"

Her sarcasm wasn't lost on him; his voice was forcibly steadied. "I'm only asking you consider it, as a last option."

"Thank you for your concern, Baldric. I'm curious, which one YOU would have bedded, as a last option, had you succeeded in becoming King. Or would you have just handed over the dragon?"

Silence filled the room to the point of bursting. Outside the window, it began to rain. She moved closer to the pane, her breath fogging her view.

Unbidden, a memory surfaced from many, many years ago.

The Andalusian sky had been thick with clouds and unspent moisture. It was late spring, or summer maybe, centuries ago. An almond grove had formed a semi-circle where she and Aniause were bound and on their knees in front of griffin shapeshifters. While two men held her, the third lifted a dull silver axe, slick with oil.

She knew she would regenerate, but still she'd trembled. Tears had filled Aniause's eyes. He'd whispered, "We are Phoenix."

It began to rain.

The axe fell.

With a violent shake of her head, Destante fought back to the present: in Mexico and alive. The war had been going on too long, and it had cost them all so much. She cleared her throat. "Gentlemen, prepare what men we have. Make a public display of them. Keep them busy and moving in and out of buildings. Confuse any spies that may be watching. Show them three and four times as many men as we have. I will call you again when I have reached any further decisions. Thank you."

She walked out, Javier and Uzdal trailing. It wasn't her problem really. She only needed to hold on until Delcinae returned. Then, her sister could deal with these headaches.

As they passed the window overlooking the outer courtyard, she pointed out a giant of a man strutting around a group of soldiers, giving orders on how to improve their swordplay. To the two men, she said, "Do you see him? That is Miguel Angél. His four brothers were tortured and killed by Noll, one-by-one, as they went searching for food. For food!"

She and Uzdal kept walking until they reached the staircase. Glancing behind, Destante saw that her *vaquero* guard, Javier, was where she'd left him: still looking out the windows. She stopped and turned fully around, staring at him.

Finally, when he returned his attention to her and began to fidget, she asked, "Do you know my past? What I am?"

He shifted uncomfortably, avoiding her gaze. "There are rumors that you are *El Diablo*. That you cannot be killed."

Destante could have laughed out loud at that. Devil? Perhaps. "I can be killed, but not easily. My enemies, however, have learned the secret to succeeding in that endeavor. One second is all it would take for someone to harm me, and if you are found looking away during that second, or if you fail me, even once, your life will not be worth having. You will be tortured so harshly, you'll beg for death. I promise you this."

His face turned a deep red, and he bowed low. "Yes, Ma'am. Forgive me. It is new to me, this ... guarding."

"You need to learn patience." She shook her finger at him.

"Impatience is my *naturaleza*."

"Then you must learn to not let it show. Ever. Impatience is a fighter's undoing."

Amusement filled his face. "Forgive me, Ma'am, but what do you know of a fighter's doing or undoing?"

"You'd be surprised." She turned away with a smile. "I have fought in battles you'd never imagine even in your dreams. Keep your guard up. Always."

# CHAPTER 15

Aniause finished smoothing the fish skin onto the boy's burnt arm. While he wrapped a bandage around the injured limb, the thought of how Destante had told him she'd been burnt. Alive most probably. He only hoped she was unconscious. The pain would have been excruciating.

If he'd known where she was, he'd have used the fish skin to help heal her. But then, he'd have had to know where she was. A pang of guilt shot through him, followed quickly by the loss that had encompassed him when she hadn't returned in a timely fashion.

The boy beneath his hand fussed and Aniause realized he'd ceased his ministrations. He concentrated on the wrap and covered it with cloth. Turning to the boy's mother, he said, "Don't take that off. Come back to me *en la mañana* so I can treat it again."

He shook his finger at the boy. "And you stay away from, *el fuego*. No fire."

Smiling, he opened the door to the waiting room and spied Pirien waiting. As the mother and boy walked past, the old man ambled into the treatment room and settled onto the table. He said, "I don't know why I have to go through this so often."

Aniause turned from the basin where he was washing. He picked up a rag and dried his hands. "Because, Pirien, you're a cranky old man and I love making you miserable."

"Well, at least we have that clear." The priest pointed at the remnants of burn treatment. "Is that fish?"

"They're using it in Brazil. I thought I'd give it a try." Aniause raised the old priest's eyelids, one after another, checking the color of the whites. Far too many red blood vessels showing.

"You drink too much."

Pirien shrugged, pursing his lips. "I'm an old man. I'm entitled at this age. And you drank as much as I did last night. More, even."

Aniause stepped back and frowned. "I'm a young man."

"Hah! You may look young, but you, my friend, are hundreds of years old."

"Open your mouth and stick out your tongue."

The older man complied, grimacing.

Peering into the back of Pirien's throat, Aniause said, "You look healthy. I'll draw some blood to check color and metals. How do you feel?"

"Fine. I feel fine."

Aniause nodded, picked up the needle and tube, and turned back to his friend.

Pirien said, "My friend, neither of us is young." His lower lip pooched in a pout as the needle slid beneath his ancient skin.

## CHAPTER 16

Destante turned toward Aniause's lab. She'd promised to speak to him after the meeting in the library. And she needed him to help her see any options that were available. Uzdal withdrew to see to his other duties. Beside her, Javier walked straighter, taller, and didn't look out the window even once. It seemed he was taking her words to heart.

As they passed through the left wing of the villa, she saw Aniause outside his exam room with Pirien. The two men spoke quietly, the young doctor animating his sentences with wide gestures. When he noticed her, he stopped. A shadow of sad regret crossed his face and he slowly turned into his exam room and shut the door.

Destante came to an abrupt halt and Javier, who'd fallen behind, sidestepped to avoid a collision. Sudden tears brimmed at the lance of pain that cut into her heart.

Aniause had rejected her.

It seemed he was sincere in his statement of ending

their relationship. He'd literally shut the door in her face. Just when she'd needed him.

A lifetime gone. Several lifetimes.

It was all too much. The changes in her life had come too quickly. She wasn't normally a crier, but her regeneration had, no doubt, left her emotional. She pivoted, blinded by hot tears that she could no longer contain. After several faltering steps toward the sanctity of her room, she picked up speed as she went. Mid-journey, she changed course and, by the time she reached the front door, she was nearly running. Tears burned down her cheeks. Her nose was getting stuffy.

She ran into the tree covered mountainside behind the villa, staggering from the sobs she tried to choke back, but that heaved her body in great wracking tidal waves anyway. She gulped in great swallows of air, just to be able to breathe. Javier followed at a distance.

When she finally stopped, could at last see clearly again, she found herself on a rocky crag that looked equally down on the villa with the backdrop of the ocean on one side and a deep hidden valley on the other. Over the centuries, it was a place she'd visited often to think over her problems.

And what a set of problems she had now! Her sister was possibly - probably - gone for good, leaving herself as the sole direct descendant in the royal line. No other carried the phoenix fire. The other nearest descendant, Baldric, was a pompous idiot who, without a fight, was willing to capitulate to neighbors who conspired against them. And as if that wasn't enough, the man she loved, her lifemate, her best friend and confidante, refused to be with her because of laws made by people no longer alive.

Actually, she should have seen that last one coming. He'd always been vocal in how he felt about her lack of interest in the affairs of the kingdom.

She should have trusted her instincts and never come home again after her rebirth. Maybe started over elsewhere. But, she'd come back for love.

Look where that had gotten her.

Destante took a deep breath and let it out slowly. Her eyes were puffy, her nose snotty, her throat raw, and she had a headache the size to split the equator. But she'd be all right.

She just needed ….

She glanced at Javier. He stood over a dozen feet away, half-facing her, flitting his gaze toward her and then looking away. He had the look of a man in panic: ready to run, but unable. Clearly her tears made him uncomfortable.

Could she trust him to keep a secret? Shaking her finger, she said, "You'll forget you ever saw this."

"Of course." He gave a half-hearted smile, then looked away again.

"I'm no devil, but what you see next is something you can repeat to no one. If you ever do, you'll wish I'd killed you here and now. Am I clear?"

He looked at her, then turned and faced her square on. "*Entiendo*."

"I sure hope you DO understand. Go to the house and get me a robe."

He crossed his arms and raised his chin in defiance. "My job is *guardia*."

She shrugged, kicked off her shoes, and focused on the phoenix within her.

Moving slowly to keep the pain at minimum, she shifted. Her arms thinned and lengthened. At the same time, her ribcage narrowed, shoving her breastplate forward, tightening the bodice of her dress. As the seams of her clothes split, Javier whirled, face aflame, to stand with his back to her. True to his word, though, he didn't leave.

Destante's face and jaw elongated into a thin, curved beak. Her feet became sharp talons. The dress fell into tatters, exposing soft down fast growing into full feathers across her body. A long plume of a tail sprouted and silky pinions covered her arms.

Where once she had been a woman, now she stood as a magnificent bird, mistress of the sky, untamed by death. A phoenix.

She gathered herself and, in a rush of power and wind, lifted off the ground. She circled. Javier stared up at her in jaw-dropping awe. Abruptly, he leaned down, scooped up her shoes, and turned toward the villa.

## CHAPTER 17

Javier's heart painfully lunged again and again against his ribs, trying to escape his chest. It pounded in his ears. He stumbled down the slope, not really aware of the trail, the queen's shoes in his hand.

What he'd seen was *imposible*.

He glanced up again, hoping for another sighting of the magnificent bird, but saw only blue sky with soft fluffy clouds. Stumbling, he jerked his attention back to his path in time to catch himself from pitching head first down the mountain.

It did little to quell his confusion, however. By the time he reached the front door of the villa, he was suspicious of everyone and everything. Who else knew about the bird? Were there others like her? Or was she the only one? He felt like he was going *loco. Muy loco*.

He entered the villa and ran up the wide marble stairs, turning the landing in front of large tiled windows, meeting up with *el doctor*.

Aniause looked further down the steps. When he returned his gaze, it was first fueled with anger, but then, perhaps seeing Javier's panic, it changed to concern. "Where's the queen? What's happened?"

Javier opened his mouth to answer, but then didn't know what to say. Would he be believed? He barely believed it himself. Surely, *el doctor* must know. With a sideways flick of his gaze to the sky outside the window, he whispered, "What is she?"

*El doctor* nodded. Didn't seem surprised. Or confused. He seemed to know exactly to what Javier referred. "She's a phoenix shapeshifter. Human, but able to become this bird."

"Not Quetzalcóatl?"

"No. She's not evil." He spoke as if it were a common everyday occurrence. Like all people, everywhere, became a bird.

Human. Not *el diablo*. Not Quetzalcóatl. Javier's panic slowed. She was a human who could become a bird. That's all.

He looked the other man up and down. "Are you? A … what? Phoenix?"

*El doctor* nodded. "As are most of us. There are many kinds of shapeshifters: snakes, crows, and bears, for example. Elis and Noll are griffins, half bird and half … jungle cat."

Javier tried to digest what he'd just heard. Elis wasn't a man either, but something else. He was an animal of some kind. Somehow it changed everything.

"She sent me for her robe." Javier lifted the queen's shoes by way of explanation. He made to move on, but the other man gripped his arm.

Aniause took the shoes. "I'll take her robe to her."

## CHAPTER 18

As the phoenix, Destante floated low over the green canopy in the depths of the canyon. Here, the acrid smoke of the volcano was trapped among the treetops. The late morning sun bore down on her and she reveled in its heated touch. The day was going to be a scorcher. She rarely flew during the daylight hours; it tended to frighten people. No birds her size were native to this area of the world.

In fact, no birds her size were native anywhere. It was widely held there had been some in Spain, centuries ago, but they'd all died out. Become extinct. Right about the time Destante's phoenix family had moved away. It was nearly true; there were so few phoenixes left.

If people only knew the truth about the shapeshifters that lived among them they'd be shocked about how many 'humans' weren't human after all.

She worked to empty her mind, concentrating on the sensations of flying, swooping low in the shadows, and brushing the ends of her wings against the branch tips she passed. She dipped even lower in the canyon, gliding among the trees. Then she flew even lower, skimming the ground and twisting and turning around the prickly needles of spruce, the tall sturdy sequoias, and the poisonous manzanillos that sprawled in her path.

It was private in the shade and she most probably wouldn't be seen, but she craved the smell of the hot salt wind blowing off the ocean instead of the sharp bite of the volcano smoke. Once again lifting out of the trees, she skimmed as phoenix up the side of the canyon and over the ridge, west toward the ocean, gaining speed as she went until she was shooting like a rocket down the ocean cliff, across the beach, and straight out over the water. Her shadow raced across the sand. Sunbathers frolicking in the surf, caught unaware, pierced the air with terrified screams.

She'd been seen. There would probably be repercussions. But nothing long lasting, she was sure.

Sailing inches above the water, far at sea and away from the burning smoke that was Colima, Destante dropped her wingtips into the ocean, sending spray high behind her. She rolled and dunked below the surface, emerging minutes later to let the wind curl through her long tail plumes. It brought to mind the times she and Aniause had flown together in the privacy of night. The tandem arcs and banks on the still warm air. Locking into an embrace as birds, plummeting into the water, then both of them shifting to human form to finish their lovemaking, buoyed by the salty waves.

His whole argument was invalid and she hadn't bothered to remind him that the fire would pass through her to the next ruler among her children, no matter whom she married. He already knew that. It had been just an excuse. She wasn't sure quite why though. She had no doubt he still loved her, but something was certainly bothering him.

It made no difference. As soon as this battle was over and she could catch a breath, she'd repeal the antiquated law of non-marriage to someone not of royal blood. It was time the phoenixes caught up to the rest of the world. Then Aniause could make a real decision.

It was high time she faced the fact that her sister wasn't coming back. If she was, she'd have done so by now. A blur of memories flooded Destante: Late giggling nights, long courtly evenings, her sister's coronation. Her sister's soulmate had died in his youth during a battle, as so many had. She'd had no Aniause. She only had Destante. They'd been best friends, even after the weight of the kingdom fell on Delcinae's shoulders.

With a violent shake of Destante's head and a savage hiss from deep in her bird throat, she drove the memories away. She concentrated instead on the fire within her. Long ago it had been in every leader of the phoenixes. Back when being a lord or lady meant something more than just owning land.

She found the spark kindling within the depths of her soul. It flickered when she came near it. Touching it brought sparks. She pulled on it. Heat flooded her body. Not burning, sizzling heat, but a warm comfortable toasty feeling. Pulling harder on it brought the flames to the surface. Every part of her body was on fire.

She stoked the flames higher, until the ocean water below her boiled as she skimmed above it.

Unbidden, the memories of Aniause returned, haunting her with the tenderness of her lover's touch, the passion in his eyes. If one of them should die permanently in battle now, unable to be reborn, their last words to each other will have been as nothing more than strangers. Saddened, she dropped the flames and turned for home and the smoke of Colima, opting to fly high above the beach area rather than startle the swimmers again. She needn't have bothered, the sand was an empty flat stretch. Apparently, the appearance of a giant bird had put an end to their relaxation.

Aniause was waiting for her, robe draped over his arm, when she approached the crag where she wanted to land. For an instant, she had the perverse idea to dive at him, hurt him like she was hurting. Then, she had the desire to fly high again, leaving and never, ever returning. She nearly did, banking sharply to the left to catch an upward draft. She didn't want to live side-by-side with him and still be strangers.

Then she circled back to land. She needed no man to make her strong, to make her whole. But she wanted to share this life with someone, and if a friend was all she could have in Aniause right now, she'd take it. But, as soon as she could, she'd make it so they could be together. Assuming he wanted it.

Instead, she spiraled down, floating on the breeze, and landed softly beside her past lover. As she shifted, he held the robe at the ready for her, eyes averted until her nakedness was covered.

With nothing left to say to each other, they returned to the villa in the silence.

When Aniause and Destante entered the front hall of the villa, they were met by Baldric, who was seeing off some guests.

Baldric hesitated when he saw Destante's robe. Glancing first to Aniause, then back to her, he said, "You flew? In the daylight?"

As Destante made to step around him, he moved between her and the stairs, effectively blocking the way. "My Queen, Elis has given Noll a prize stallion. The treaty will be signed soon. We must have an answer. "

He began to pace. When he spoke again, it was with the familiar usage of her name. "Destante, we run the risk of ruination at the hands of these two men, and yet you do nothing about it. It's as if you don't care if your father's kingdom is destroyed. Just make the decision. It's a simple matter."

He stopped and watched her, his mouth open a bit, as if to help her form the words. "Do you mean us to be overtaken by these two fiends?"

Aniause interrupted, "The queen is still recovering from her rebirth. Your bullying will only have an adverse affect."

He held up a hand when Baldric began to speak. "She needs complete peace right now. Your questions will keep."

Again, Baldric looked ready to speak, but Aniause cut him off with a firm, "They will keep."

A dark scowl filled Baldric's face and he stormed away.

When they were alone, Aniause turned and stiffly left.

Destante watched until he was out of sight, her heart battering her ribs, urging her to follow. He'd looked at her as if she was suddenly no one he'd ever cared about. But she'd also seen the hidden spark of anger when he realized Baldric wasn't going to stop pushing.

It was a comfort, but not much.

# CHAPTER 19

Elis paced his throne room, shaking his head and muttering to himself. The servants stood silently at the edge of the room, wide-eyed, ready to bolt, like frightened deer rooted to the spot until the predator noticed them. They knew not to disturb him in moments like that.

He beckoned to one of them, who approached nearly on the run and stood with bowed head. He might have even been shaking.

"Bring Cardenas. He waits outside the door." Elis flicked his fingers by way of dismissal.

He'd had the phoenixes within his grasp. Not just them, but also the last dragon alive. He would have ended the thousand-year war in one fatal swoop and been lauded a hero.

Then, in one heartbeat, Destante had put an end to his plans.

No, he corrected. Not an end, just a pause. The

outcome would be the same.

Elis smiled at the thought and looked up at the approaching Cardenas. The mercenary was tall and lean with a cruel twist to his mouth. Maliciousness glinted in his eyes. He returned the king's smile and then, perhaps realizing the smile wasn't for him, slowly dropped to one knee, head bowed.

Elis said, "The queen of the phoenixes needs a gentle reminder she is an insignificant power. Take my son and visit her in her home. Invent a pretext. Make your warning clear."

Cardenas carefully said, head still bowed, "Sire, your son –"

"He needs to grow stronger. He won't, if he's kept out of the transactions that make a kingdom great. Take him under your care. Teach him the ways of power."

"Yes, Sire." Cardenas rose and strode out of the room in long strides.

## CHAPTER 20

That evening, Destante sipped her pulque in the darkness of the hacienda. When her father had first moved his family across the ocean to this wild country, she'd turned her nose up at the thick, sour drink made from agave plants. There had been nothing like it in Spain. Now, it was like a balm on her aching heart. Comfort. Like the twinkling lights of boats on the ocean that merged with the glittering stars in the night sky, as if she was in a bubble of fireflies that twinkled their best to try to cheer her broken heart.

A warm wind softly blew in from over the water, bringing with it the taste of salt in the air and the scent of all creatures marine, blowing the smoke of the volcano away from them. A refreshing change. Crickets and owls serenaded her from all sides.

Even through her sorrow, her head was spinning the problem of Noll and Elis around and around, seeking for an answer that hadn't been seen before. Noll was stronger than Elis. But, Elis was the initiator. Why would they align instead of just destroying her, and those she held dear?

What about Elis? If she aligned with him, would the two of them be strong enough to hold off Noll? Is that what had happened with Delcinae? Instead of Baldric assassinating her, perhaps she'd aligned with Elis.

Noll, fearing a united power against him that was strong enough to overthrow him, may have decided to forego any take-over plans and had killed Delicinae.

It was no accident that this treaty between Noll and Elis appeared when the queen went missing and the money and favors stopped flowing. Griffins, both, she didn't think either would be willing to ally themselves with her kingdom again, no matter what was offered.

How had they found out about the dragon shapeshifter? Someone in the royal family had to have told them. She was surrounded by traitors. Baldric came first to her mind. No doubt some of the other lords were loyal to Elis. Then there was possibility, probability, of Javier being a traitor, no matter what Aniause believed.

A ghost moved across the yard to her left, came closer, materialized to be Pirien. He pulled out a seat beside her and dropped into it with a weary huff, assembling his priest's robes around him.

She poured a second goblet of pulque from the flask and handed it to him. Of all the people in her kingdom, this was one man she could trust. Her father had taught her that.

Pirien took the goblet and thanked her with a wave of his hand.

They sat that way, silent, sipping the thick white drink. Destante closed her eyes, the night sounds flowing through her. To save her kingdom, her people, her family, and the dragon, she could uproot everyone and move them, as her father had when the dragon had first come to them.

But did she want to do that? She loved this place. It had become her home: the ocean, the hot white sun, the thick stemmed vegetation that sometimes didn't want to grow through the rocky ground.

Pirien finished his drink and stood, staring out over the black of the ocean. After a moment, he softly said, "The dragons started the war. Did you know that?"

She nodded. "I did. My father was in the dragon's castle as emissary. But he wouldn't tell me the full story. Do you know the truth of what happened?"

"The dragons have a secret and they guard it with every fiber of their being. The woman, a young witch, discovered their truth and was given a choice between living with the dragons for the rest of her life –"

"Or choose death."

The ancient priest turned to face Destante. "She chose death. However, a young griffin was madly in love with her and was determined to rescue her. The fight between he and the dragon prince went badly for the griffin until the witch broke free and killed the dragon prince. There has been war ever since."

"And the dragons tell everyone it was a love triangle to continue to protect the secret that the witch discovered."

Pirien nodded sadly. "It's a sad story and it shouldn't have led to war, but the dragon king was so heart-broken over the loss of his son, he vowed to find the two young lovers any way possible. When he couldn't find them, he declared war, hoping to kill them in the ensuing battles."

"Did he?"

"Yes, but by then the war had a life of its own and couldn't be stopped. Though he contains no magical powers, the young king, Elis, is a descendent of that couple. He will never quit seeking his own vengeance." He waved his thanks and slowly ambled back the way he'd come, looking like a ghost again, to disappear in the dark.

She bolted down the last of her drink and reached for the flask. Finding it empty, she turned her goblet upside down on the table. She'd had enough anyway.

She couldn't make any decisions about Noll and Elis based on the few facts she had. More information was required. Raising her voice, she spoke to the shadow leaning against the wall to her right. "Javier, pick out a small, gentle mare from the stables for me to ride. Make sure she is well shod and sound on the rough trails. We'll leave on a tour of the countryside in the morning. Also, send for Aniause and Baldric, please."

Within moments after he left, Aniause appeared. His voice was guarded. Stiff. "Javier said you asked for me?"

"Tomorrow morning, you will accompany me on a riding tour of the kingdom."

Aniause frowned and opened his mouth to speak, but she put up her hand to ward him off. "I understand your need to avoid me, but like it or not, yours is one of the few voices around here I trust. You're stuck with me."

Baldric appeared, escorted by a grim Javier. No doubt her bodyguard had taken some abuse at the hands of her cousin.

She said, "Cousin, I've given careful consideration to this topic of the treaty between Noll and Elis. And I've decided I don't know enough to make any decisions. I need to find out more before I can decide about them."

"With all due respect, Elis won't —"

" — He will have everything in place for the treaty,

but will wait to see if I decide to hand over the dragon, knowing that I will have heard about his plans. I suspect he's no fool, and would rather take this kingdom without bloodshed. He will wait, and I will give him reason to wait."

"But —"

"My decision is made, Baldric. I want you here early in the morning wearing riding clothes."

He bowed and left, a dark scowl on his face.

"Javier, please have our financial records sent to me."

"Tonight?"

"Yes. Tonight."

# CHAPTER 21

Aniause found himself unable to stop his smile, watching Destante order Baldric around. Order them all around.

He'd failed. It hadn't even been a day since his grandiose speech, yet here he was, grinning like a giddy, love-sick, school boy.

Such as it had always been where Destante was concerned.

A memory pushed forward. They'd been very young and had fought in their first battle, not yet a mated pair. She'd been killed in battle, crashing to the ground through the thick clouds they fought in. He didn't see she was gone at first, distracted by his own enemies. When he'd finally noticed she wasn't near, he'd wasted valuable time searching the clouds. At last his deepest fears finally forced him to inspect the ground, where he found her laying in a bone-broken pile, dead.

He'd pulled her into a secluded rock outcropping. And had been nearly unable to breathe, holding her for what seemed an eternity, until, at last, a slow blush crept through her skin. Her chest rose with a first breath. With a great whoosh of relief, he'd quickly rearranged her body, lining up the bones where they should have been, holding some while they mended.

It took days.

He'd never left her side. The battle raged above and around him. Once, a wolf shifter dared peek his head into where they were hiding. Aniause had shifted to phoenix and dispatched him without a second glance.

At last, she opened her eyes.

Then and there he declared his love for her, pledging himself to her side for as long as they lived. With happy tears, she pledged to him as well, and, when she was whole again, they consummated their love in that rock outcropping.

For hundreds of years, he'd been in love with her and his heart wouldn't be quiet now. No matter the necessity. Nor how much he scolded it.

He shouldn't have gone up to the peak of the cliff with her robe. Shouldn't have seen her sleek naked body in the warm sunlight. He'd been playing with fire and he'd known it. But, he'd known she was there because of him. He couldn't stand her heartbreak and that's why he'd gone.

He also knew he'd been right in his speech that morning.

And he and Pirien had been right about her being a better choice than her cousin. She was already proving it.

Destante led him to the dining hall. "I need your help understanding how much money flowed to whom and how regularly."

Aniause shrugged. "I'm a doctor. I never understood numbers." In fact, he did. He just hated math. Especially money.

She narrowed her eyes and glared, her hands on her hips. "Well Doctor, let me put this in terms you'll understand. Your patient is gravely ill. In fact, he might die if we can't find the infection that threatens him. His symptoms are a serious lack of funds and a festering traitor. Does that work for you?"

Ignoring the sarcasm dripping from her voice, he pulled out a heavy chair and reached for the ledger. Destante snugged up a chair near his and leaned in over the next ledger. They studied the finances for a long time until she slid her ledger on top of his.

"There appears to be no entries titled, "bribe". But look here." She jabbed her forefinger at an entry. Her knee pressed against his, her shoulder against his. The heat from her body stove the fire in his own, making his mind foggy. Her natural scent teased his sensitive phoenix senses. She said, "This deduction comes regularly out of the account. Quite frequently, in fact. It seems pretty vague. 'Contract services rendered'. What's that mean? Why wouldn't they put it plainly as a bribe?"

He leaned over her ledger and shook his head. "It's a large amount. I have that in my ledger, too."

They both leaned back in their chairs. She nodded. "We know how much, and how regularly. Just not to whom."

Aniause shook his head again and straightened his stiff back. They'd been hunched over the ledgers, searching for clues for over an hour. They were no closer to finding the traitor than when they'd started. With misgivings, he stood. He really hated leaving her, hated going back to his own empty room. He didn't even try to hide the regret. "Goodnight. Sleep well."

She appeared not to have noticed his words. Her

gaze was fixed on an unseen distance. He knew that look all too well. She'd hit on an idea and would follow it to the very end. And if it came up fruitless, she'd start on it again. She slowly turned to him, focused, and said, "Baldric is probably the one to speak with. I probably shouldn't have let him out of his cell yet. I just don't trust him."

He nodded. "You're right. But we're not going to figure it out tonight. Go to sleep. We'll have a long ride tomorrow." He turned to go, knowing she'd likely be up all night, following her ideas.

He passed the room where Baldric was quartered. Halfway down the hall, Aniause doubled back to Baldric's door and rapped his knuckles on the time-smoothed wood.

Baldric was still in full dress when he answered, unusual for so late an hour. His brow was heavy, mirroring his scowl. "What is it?"

"I need a word with you. May I come in?"

"What you need to say can be spoken from out there."

"If you wish, but I rather thought you'd prefer the matter of your betrayal to be spoken of quietly. Not brought up again and again for the people to remember." Aniause shrugged.

Baldric swung the door wide and, with sarcasm thick in his voice, said, "Won't you please come in, honored guest."

Shaking his finger at the lord as he stepped past into the room, Aniause said, "No need for hostilities."

Shutting the door, Baldric turned, his fists clenched. "What exactly should there be, considering everyone believes me a traitor?"

"Are you not? Killing the queen and her sister?" Anger simmered inside Aniause.

Shock lit across Baldric's face. "I had nothing to do with the queen's death."

"But the sister?"

He shook his head and began to pace the spacious room. Aniause followed him with his gaze. Though under doubt, Destante had given her cousin quarters due his rank. "I didn't kill her."

"You separated her head from her body?"

Baldric paused near the window and took a deep sigh. "It was already removed. I was only to keep her from being reborn."

"And assume the throne."

He nodded slowly, narrowing his gaze. Waiting.

Aniause swallowed the building fury. He had to find out the truth. "To what end?"

Baldric shrugged like his answer was obvious. "To save our people. There's no need for more to die, no need for us to give up our homes. We have the last dragon. The very last. Their race is already dead."

"So you told Elis about the dragon and offered it up." Aniause wasn't asking a question. It was a blatant accusation. Now his own fists clenched, his nails digging deep into his palms.

"He knew already. Someone told him. He was ready to kill us all," Baldric said sadly. He dropped into a chair, his head in his hands.

CHAPTER 22

The next morning, Destante stared out over the ocean, perched in a chair on her hacienda, snuggled in a blanket. She'd been there most of the night. It was now nearly midmorning, but it would be several hours before the long shadows of the mountain behind her would allow sunlight and warmth where Destante sat.

The wind was still blowing from the sea, still driving the stench of Colima away, but rumblings deep in the earth continued, strengthening.

The villa behind her stirred with rustlings and mutterings of people going about their morning business. There were a couple straggling guests, packing in preparation for their return home, but most were employees just settling into their day. To her right, a silent Javier had relieved the night guard and was leaning against the wall of the building in his usual spot, yawns heavy upon him.

Aniause walked toward her from his room in the far wing of the house. He yawned and stretched his arms overhead. Settling into the seat beside her, he asked, "Up all night?" His voice was soft, like it always was when he woke late.

She said, "The problem remains. Who's been getting the money? Both Noll and Elis have plenty. And this is a war about loyalties. I find it hard to believe they would want money. The question has been rolling round and round in my head all night, but I'm no closer to an answer now than when I started."

He stretched again. "The same could be said for your extended family. They have plenty of money. You'll figure it out. I have no doubt."

"I think I first need to find out who's living beyond their means."

"Is that why we're traveling on horseback all over the countryside today?"

"Partly, yes. The other part is I want people to see me. To make a statement to everyone, including Elis and Noll, who will, no doubt, get word somehow that I'm unafraid. "

Behind Aniause, Javier straightened and stared at the villa door. Destante turned. Adelita entered the courtyard with two mustached men. The size of the two men dwarfed the maid. One was a tall Mexican with an ugly sneer on his face, and the other was a broad European, but neither was someone Destante had seen before.

Both men carried long black machetes strapped over their backs, and had apologetic smiles on their faces. The tall Mexican seemed to be in charge; he had an air of authority when he spoke. "I'm sorry to disturb you at this time of morning. I am Alejandro Luis Cardenas."

He paused suddenly and stared out over the ocean. "This is the most beautiful view I have ever seen."

He took a deep breath and slowly exhaled, standing with his hands on his hips for several minutes. Eventually he turned his attention back to Destante. "There are rumors of a giant bird in this area"

She shook her head. "I've been away. I returned two days ago."

"It was seen yesterday. There." He motioned in the direction of the beach she'd flown over.

"Ah." Destante nodded. "I've had guests and have been busy with them. I've seen no bird."

"Over the next few days," Cardenas continued, "we will be scouting the hills, searching for it."

He shook his finger at her. "For your own safety, do not leave your home. I will come tell you when it is safe again." He smiled, gave a quick nod of goodbye, and then turned to go, the machete making his statement more than a concern for her safety.

Due to the shadows from the mountain behind them, Destante was able to watch through the villa windows as the two men walked into, and then through the building. They did not stop, nor did they look around much more than a cursory glance. They mounted their horses and galloped away.

Aniause said, "He knows what we are."

"Yes he does." She pursed her lips and turned to Javier, who had settled into his lean again. "Please go saddle our horses."

Shock rippled across his face and he rose off the wall. His gaze shifted rapidly to Aniause, then back to her.

Destante scowled. "Don't look at him. He can't help you change my mind."

With a shrug, Javier loped off across the yard toward the stables as Baldric approached from the villa.

Aniause frowned and said, "Destante, are you sure

you want to go riding around the countryside right now? It's dangerous. You heard Cardenas. There's no doubt that was a threat."

She laughed. "What's wrong? Is the itty bitty phoenix afraid he might get hurt?"

His face clouded momentarily, and then cleared. He smiled like the rogue she remembered of old. "Well, if you put it that way...."

CHAPTER 23

Destante reined in her bay mare and studied the steep hillsides and rocky terrain. Any trees nearby were far back from the path, offering no shelter from the burn of the sun. Some of the smaller settlements were only a few families and had foot trails for access, not roads for carts and wagons. In front of her rode Javier, picking the best route for the horses and keeping an eye out for danger. Aniause rode beside her, when space allowed. Baldric followed behind, and behind him were the two *guardias* Uzdal had insisted on sending.

They were headed east, in the direction of Elis and Colima.

She'd refused Adelita's accompaniment, though she knew the young girl would endure the ride well. She had another plan in mind.

She turned and spoke over her shoulder. "Aniause, where are the people? I haven't seen many all day." Sweat rolled off her in sheets and her stomach rumbled. They'd only stopped once, for the noon *almuerzo*. That had been hours ago.

The doctor urged his mount forward, coming abreast of her. "They've probably heard the rumor of an upcoming battle and, coupled with the rumblings from Colima, have left while they could."

"Who owns this property?"

"Balteus."

Destante frowned. "I didn't realize we'd crossed into his territory yet. I would think he would be concerned enough about his people to reassure them." She nudged her mare to continue up the steep incline of the hillside, but her horse stumbled, nearly sending them both onto the rocky path. She caught her breath in her throat, her heart racing from the near catastrophe. Then she reined up again to calm her nerves, once more halting the party behind her. Perhaps they'd be better off leading the horses. But glancing ahead, she saw that Javier kept his horse climbing up the hillside. He knew this terrain better than any of them. If he felt safe riding, then they'd ride.

She motioned Aniause ahead to speak to Baldric. "How many people are left in this region?"

His dark eyes flashed at her. In a tight voice, he said, "I'm not my brother. I don't know."

Destante turned her back on him. She should have known he'd be no help. She shouted at her guard's back. "Javier!"

He stopped his mount and twisted in his saddle to face her.

She said, "Wait there for me. I would like to speak with you."

He moved his horse to the side of the trail to let the others pass, but Aniause halted as well. When she reached Javier, he fell in beside her, Aniause following. She said, "Tell me of the other two regions between here and Elis. Are they as devoid of people as this one?"

"The next one, owned by Lord Torag, *es abandonado*. The farther one *pertenece* — belongs— to Lord Sharoth. It borders Elis's land. The people may have left it as well. But I don't know. I haven't been that far in quite some time."

She glanced behind her, at Aniause. "Tonight, we'll take a look at the treasury records again."

"Happily."

They fell into silence while Destante thought over what she'd learned. The people were leaving the area, yet no one of her family seemed concerned. They should be recruiting soldiers for the upcoming battle from the people instead of letting them leave.

Eventually, the land softened into a more hospitable ride and a large sprawling villa appeared on the hillside above them. It had three flags raised above the entrance: Mexican, Phoenix, and a third with a blue and gold star.

"Tell me something, Javier. What flag is that last one?"

His face flushed. "It is Elis's."

Anger lit across Destante like a white hot bolt of lightning. Perhaps seeing it on her face, Aniause broke in. "Many along the borders fly both flags, to keep Elis and Noll at bay."

She marshaled her temper under control. These people were scared, but if there was fighting here, flags wouldn't keep her family safe. Nor those under her protection. And certainly not the dragon.

Balteus, himself, approached from the villa. He focused briefly on his twin, Baldric, and sneered. Recovering quickly, he turned to her, bowed, and said, "My Queen, we were unaware of your visit."

Destante hadn't missed the quickly covered hatred toward his sibling. She said, "I am merely touring the borderlands. I wish to be no bother."

"It would grace me to have you within my walls. And, as it's a long ride back to your own villa, stay for the evening meal. Then, if it pleases you, stay for the night."

"Thank you, Balteus. I think we'll take advantage of your hospitality." She dismounted, handing her horse to a waiting servant. Walking toward the villa, she twisted one way and then another, stretching her sore muscles. It had been since long before her recent death and rebirth that she'd ridden and her legs were already aching.

CHAPTER 24

Entering Balteus's villa was like visiting an oasis in the midst of a desert. Destante walked directly into a lush courtyard, complete with a fountain-adorned pond. Well-fleshed guards in dark green European style uniforms held long swords and lurked among the tropical plants. Fat servants peopled the open space. Cool waves of air came from small windows strategically built into the hacienda's walls between nooks of marble and gold statuary. Everywhere she looked was opulence.

She was shown to a bed chamber heavy in silver and turquoise trimmings where she washed away the travel grime at a marbled basin. Her parched skin drank in the cool water and the tensions of the day washed into the bottom of the bowl. She would have loved a bath, but there wasn't time.

Balteus himself seated her at the head of a silver trimmed table. A good half of the places intended for her company were still empty; she wasn't the only one dawdling. A modestly dressed servant brought her spiced tea mixed with cold, fresh fruit. She slowly sipped the drink, while listening to Balteus's ingratiating prattle. As soon as her drink was half gone, a servant refilled it. One by one, her retinue filtered into the room and settled into their places.

As soon as Balteus's wife arrived, waves of servants brought in the meal. Thick, rich sauces cooked with fruit were layered over trays of meat and fish. Bowls piled high with spiced vegetables made the rounds. Gilded rose petals highlighted desserts piled on crystal plates. Copious scraps fell to obese dogs under the table.

The threat of Elis and volcano appeared to mean nothing to these people. Then, perhaps Elis was not a threat to them at all. Perhaps he was their friend.

Volumes of discussion surrounded the table amidst the tinks of crystal and clatter of silver utensils on silver plates.

Destante asked Balteus, "What do you think of this threat of battle?"

She could have imagined it, but it seemed as though the sound level in the room dropped and all present leaned in to hear his answer.

He didn't hesitate. "It's all bluff, I'm sure."

"But if it isn't, what would you do, were you in my shoes?"

He slowly glanced around the overburdened table. "I think there are very few of our clan left. A battle will only deplete our numbers more. It is the last dragon. That clan's epitaph has already been written. Let Elis come take it."

"So you would hand it over?"

"I would let it take its chances with Elis. If it escapes, it's not our problem."

"Our people would become Elis's subjects. Our

lands would become his."

Balteus shrugged. "We would all be alive."

She nodded. Most of her council probably felt the same and, glancing around the table, she saw it was true of many of those present. Some notable exceptions: Baldric and Aniause, who both wore masks of fury.

She knew why Aniause was angry, he'd never let anyone have the dragon, but she couldn't understand Baldric's attitude. He was the one who'd tried to usurp the throne, after all. What was his game?

She studied Balteus again. Was he the traitor? Had he been the one to tell Elis about the dragon?

CHAPTER 25

Aniause watched a flurry of emotions run across Destante's face. Shock, anger, understanding, back to anger. Then her eyes slowly narrowed into suspicion.

He understood that last all too well. Balteus would be in a prime position to tell Elis about the dragon. But if Aniause were to find out the truth, he'd have to trap the phoenix lord. Perhaps he could pretend to agree.

Waiting until the meal had finished and Destante had left for her room, pleading a headache, he moved to sit beside Balteus. He spoke quietly so others wouldn't interrupt. "Lord Balteus, I commend you on your position concerning Elis and the dragon."

The phoenix lord called for the servants to fill their goblets again and smiled ruefully. "I'm surprised to hear that from you, given your past relationship with your queen. It's not very popular opinion with her, I'm afraid."

"When she became queen, I fell to the wayside." The use of 'your queen' didn't escape Aniause's notice. Balteus had already chosen Elis's side.

The lord studied his drink, and continued as if speaking to the liquor. "Well, she's young and new to the throne. She'll see I'm right. And she might even return to you."

Aniause answered, "Hopefully she'll reach both understandings before Elis decides to take matters into his own hands."

"Indeed."

"Of course, she was right about one thing: Elis will seize our lands and add them to his own. He'll install his own trusted lords instead, to rule over the property."

"Not all lords will be replaced." Balteus raised his gaze and smiled.

"So, in turn for telling him about the dragon, he will let you keep your lands and title. That's quite a strategy." Aniause raised his goblet as a toast.

They drank deeply.

Balteus settled his goblet carefully on the table, frowning. "I wish I could take credit, but Elis already knew about the dragon when I spoke to him."

CHAPTER 26

Destante fumed in her room after dinner. Balteus and wife had turned the whole meal into a party, as if there wasn't a care in the world. As if they had all the funds in the world. The festivities were still going on, but she'd fled, pleading tiredness and a headache. She'd locked her bedroom door as soon as she'd arrived back there.

With a deep exasperated sigh, she settled against the headboard of her bed and opened the financial ledgers. Now that she knew what to look for, the fraudulent entries were obvious. It seemed her sister had been quite free with the money to quiet tongues. No wonder they had no funds left.

She'd been that way ever since they were children, preferring to placate than to stand up for what she believed. It had caused many a rift between the two of them until Destante grew weary of being angry and let Delcinae off the hook.

The question remained:  Who had betrayed them?

Who had told Elis about the dragon?

She still didn't trust Javier or Baldric. Now she had Balteus on the list, as well.

She cursed and stared at the figures, mentally adding and subtracting. The final numbers staggered her. The total was quite heavy. She should have twelve times as much in her accounts as she did. Of course, she'd have to wait until she got back home to figure out the exact numbers.

A knock on her door pulled her attention away. She set her current ledger aside and walked to the door, still thinking. Perhaps a good inventory of everything within her properties was in order.

She opened the door to reveal Aniause.

He stepped past her into the room. "That was quite a meal, wasn't it?"

"Yes, it was. Quite excessive." She walked to the window and stared out at the open courtyard where several of the thick-waisted servants were slowly cleaning the dishes away.

He joined her. "I rather get the impression they feast like that frequently."

"It saddens me. Technically, they've done nothing wrong. But, they know our kingdom is in financial trouble and with a battle coming. The money they spent tonight could have fed a lot of people, hired quite a few soldiers."

"I spoke with Balteus after you left. It's true, what he said. He intended to let Elis waltz right through our lands and take the dragon. But he wasn't the one who told him about it. Baldric, either. Both claim Elis already knew."

"Can we believe them?"

"I don't think either was lying. Baldric was truly distressed and Balteus is too arrogant to not brag if he'd done it."

She frowned. She'd been so sure it had been Baldric, especially after making his claim on the throne. If neither lord was lying, then she had someone else to worry about. Exactly how many traitors did she have in her kingdom?

After a moment of silence, Aniause quietly asked, "What do we do?"

Destante stared out the window. "We do nothing. Not yet."

Aniause's face turned a deep crimson, and his eyes darkened in anger. His voice was low and sounded constrained when he spoke. "May I ask your reasons?"

"I suspect there are many people like Balteus within the borders of our kingdom. If I take him to task now, the others will hear of it. They'll hide their corruption and we'll never see the truth."

She looked out at the encroaching darkness. "It grieves me though, knowing these people would rather join Elis than protect the dragon. But our subterfuge and temporary silence will enable us to root out the traitors in our midst."

"You have a plan then?"

"Not entirely yet, but I know we'll have to act quickly and all at once, rather than bit by bit. For now, we must lull them into a false security." She turned back to him and shrugged. "On the topic of the bribes, I'm just beginning to learn how much we've lost. But as I said earlier, I see no reason for anyone of the phoenix shifters to have received any money. I don't think any of them would have betrayed the dragon, either. And they're all quite wealthy after living hundreds of years. Even Torag, after inheriting from generations in his family. I have no idea who could be involved."

"So for now we just play along?"

She nodded. "Yes. I think, though, we'll start recruiting men for our army once we return home."

"Why not do it as we ride?"

"Perhaps, but not until the end of our journey. I don't want Elis and Noll hearing of it until we're ready. They could decide to attack early. So, when we do begin recruiting, it will mean taking men only from the center of our kingdom. Then, once we're strong enough, we'll move to the outer regions. I'd rather they thought of me weak and ineffectual until the moment we prove otherwise."

He nodded. "I have to say I didn't see many men today. Did you?"

She shook her head. "Just the ones here."

He sighed. "I suppose we'll find some, sooner or later. How do you propose to pay for your soldiers with no money in our coffers?"

Destante leaned back and looked up at him. "We actually have a little money. I think it will carry us until we can recoup what we lost. We'll be able to pay the soldiers."

"Your current soldiers will be angry and may quit if others are given the same amount as them. They've been working a long time without decent wages."

"That's something we'll have to rectify as soon as we get back. We may have to pay our new recruits less for a short while."

"And when the money is gone?"

"There will be more. I have a few ideas."

Aniause hesitated and looked at her, and then shook his head. "It may work, but not many men will leave their families. Theirs is the only source of income."

"One problem at a time, please."

CHAPTER 27

In the morning, Aniause waited on his patient gelding, watching Destante with Balteus and his wife. She was laying it a bit too thick for his tastes.

She said, "Last night's feast was spectacular. Not many could have done better. You brought out your best for me, and you have my thanks." The smile she gave looked forced, though, to him.

Their host appeared not to have noticed it wasn't genuine. He flushed and bowed. His wife curtseyed. "Thank you, My Queen."

Destante continued, "I see that you have a very impressive set of guards. That's good, as close as you are to Elis's border. I hope you keep a tight rein on what's left of the local population. We don't need them crossing the river and joining the griffins."

"They're a difficult bunch, but I have them well in hand."

"Indeed. Good day. Until we meet again." Destante turned her mare and headed up the road. Aniause nodded to Balteus, noting the scowl he tried to hide while watching his twin brother, Baldric, ride away.

Aniause hurried to catch Destante and sidled his horse up to hers. Their knees bumped, and his heart thudded. Would he never get over his feelings for her? "Do you think you overdid it with Balteus? He's no fool."

"Fool, no. Traitor, yes. But I think they bought it, don't you? Tell me about Sharoth. I haven't had much to do with him."

"As I know him, he's a good man. Loyal to you."

"I'm a bit skeptical about that. How can he be loyal, lying dead center of a triangle between Balteus, Torag, and Elis?"

Aniause shrugged. "I don't know. But he has little to do with them. In the court, he appears decent."

"We shall see."

CHAPTER 28

Leaving Balteus, Destante and her retinue rode into the corner of Sharoth's, passing through more tiny, empty settlements and abandoned hillside farms. They rode further into the mountains, closer to Volcán de Fuego, Colima, and it's twin, Nevado de Colima. Climbing was steep and they had to traverse carefully. Here, the smoke hung heavy in the air and wide gashes in the rocky ground spewed hot steam and noxious gases. Breathing was difficult and the horses fought to escape the fumes with every stride.

At last, they began a slow, careful descent into a green valley, moving beneath the thick smoke clouds. Sharoth's region was a long and narrow strip separating the two phoenix lords, Balteus and Torag, from the griffin king, Elis. Looking across the valley, toward Elis's kingdom, she could make out a dark line of greenery. The river that divided the two kingdoms.

Destante turned her horse toward it. "If I remember correctly, this is a critical crossing into Elis's land. I need to see it."

Javier's eyes widened and his face blanched. He shook his head violently and wouldn't meet her gaze. "It is *peligroso*, dangerous, by the river. *Los bandidos* wander its shores to rob travelers. Most are killed."

She narrowed her gaze. What made him so nervous? Was it really just concern for her safety? Or something more? The closer they'd come to Elis's property line, the more jittery he'd become. She said, "There may be thieves, but I still need to see it."

His brow burrowed itself into a dark frown, but he led the way to a crag of rocks, Aniause, Baldric, and the other two guards trailing behind. Once there, they all dismounted and crouched low behind a thick stand of shrubs, watching the riverside.

Her bodyguard pointed at the other side of the river. "There are *lanzas* stabbed into the ground, all along in front of *los arboles* — the trees."

Destante looked at where he was pointing. If he hadn't pointed them out, she might not have seen them. She traced the line with her gaze and came upon a long section of pikes capped with the heads of men, women, and even children.

The heads were wide-mouthed, staring. Blood in fat streaks of black coated the pikes of the older beheadings, red down the newer ones.

Now she knew what was happening to all the local people. What few that were still alive were fleeing Elis's *bandidos*. What she was seeing was obviously sanctioned by him. So, why hadn't he attacked yet? This was an act of a man getting ready to fight.

Movement along her side of the river caught her attention. A small group of five men came into view, two on horseback, the rest on foot, their right legs bound to a rope stretched between the two horses.

One of the two mounted men was the same who'd

earlier come into her home: Cardenas! She squinted, trying to make out the features of the other rider. Was he the European who'd visited her? He had to be, didn't he?

The riders dismounted and pulled long machetes out of leather saddle scabbards. With quick strokes, they cut off the heads of the three bound men, and then rolled the bodies into the water to bob downstream. Remounting, they rode across the river and piked the heads.

Rage rolled across Destante. Her hands were shaking and her vision was red at the edges. Not only had those men killed people from within her own borders, but it was patently obvious they worked for Elis. She now had proof he was warning people away from fighting for her. All her recruiting would come to nothing. The only people she could depend upon were the ones she already had. Time to make a new plan.

One thought kept intruding, though. Elis had sent his own men into her home.

She stood and slowly walked back to her horse. An idea was forming. She mounted and twisted around in her seat, pleased to find Baldric pale. "Aniause told me of your plan to hand over the dragon in recompense of saving our people. After what we've seen here, do you really think he'd have honored his half of the agreement?"

Baldric stared at her. His mouth opened to speak, but closed again. Once more it opened and closed. Like a fish gasping for water. A drowning man.

She nodded, satisfied. He may still betray her, but not with Elis, now that he knew the true nature of the griffin king. "I need you to find maps of our kingdom along the river. Even before we rest. As a matter of fact, bring me maps of ALL our land owners, no matter where they are located.”

He blinked hard and spoke in a subdued voice. “Yes, My Queen. I will do all that. But for now, the nearness of these men concerns me. Please, wait here until I return. I will make sure our way is safe.”

Baldric motioned to Javier and one of his guards. They galloped down the path and around a bend.

Destante narrowed her gaze and waited until the slow count of ten. Then she urged her mare into a gallop after the group.

“Destante!” Aniause and his horse caught up to her. The remaining guard close behind.

“If someone were to ambush us, one way is to wait until our guards left to check the road ahead. We’re safe; no one will be expecting this. Besides, who says Javier isn’t one of them. He’s hiding something. I don’t trust either him or Baldric yet.”

CHAPTER 29

They rounded the bend in the road and found Javier and his men locked in a combat with a large group of *bandidos*. Sword and machete clanged against knife and bar. Horses grunted, rearing high in the air and pivoting to come down on top of ground-bound men. The guard who had been left behind with Destante joined into the battle.

Javier's face had transformed into a vicious mask, and he swung his blade with cruel precision, felling all who stood in his way. Uzdal had trained him well in swordwork. The bandits taunted him by name.

Baldric was fighting like a madman, feinting left and right, stabbing more than cutting, as in the ways of the Spanish courts where he'd grown up. Men fell.

She smiled. She'd always loved a good fight, and had been too long since she'd been in one. This fight, though small, promised to be fun. She didn't see Cardenas, nor the other man from the river, so she pushed her horse forward. A tall bandit with a cloth across the bottom of his face backed away from the hacking melee. As he turned around, she brought her foot crashing into his neck, crushing his throat. He dropped to the ground like a 500 pound weight, clawing at his neck. Jumping from her horse, she snatched up his pike, stepped up behind the next man, and drove the pike into his lower spine. As he fell forward, one of the guards sliced off his head.

And then Aniause was beside her, pulling her away. "Come out of there, you'll get hurt!"

"Do you forget what we are? Who we are? What we've done? Why should we be afraid? We've fought worse. Don't you miss this?"

He hesitated, a wistful shadow crossing his face. Then he shook it away. "You're not the same person you once were. You're the queen now. You may be reborn, but remember the consequences if you die. This is a critical juncture. What will happen to your people? Who will lead them? What about Elis?"

He glanced at Baldric, who had remounted and now slashed left and right from his horse. "The kingdom will go to him. Is that what you want?"

Destante paused. For the first time, it really hit her. Delcinae wasn't coming back. Ever. It had been far too long. Until now, she'd held onto the smallest, hidden hope of her sister's return. But it was just hope. Not reality. If Destante wasn't to be ruler of the phoenixes, then Baldric would be. Or Balteus. Consequences indeed.

Either one of them could, doubtless, handle the throne during peacetime. Most any fool could. But now? When so much was at stake? Her people deserved better than either one of those two. They deserved better than a dead queen.

She let Aniause pull her to the bay mare, and she remounted to watch from the hillside above. "If we go to battle with Elis, I WILL be fighting. Everyone will. No arguments." She stabbed her finger at him to make her point clear.

He nodded. "As it always has been; royalty leads the way."

Javier, Baldric, and the guards finished off the bandits within a few minutes. The guard who'd beheaded the men Destante had dispatched walked over to Javier and spoke to him in a low voice. Her bodyguard lifted his gaze to her, fire flashing in his eyes.

The guard contingency remounted and, as Javier rode beside Destante, his jaw was clenched, his back was stiff. He spoke to no one. The minute they stopped for the noon repast, he peeled his horse away from the group and barked orders at his men.

Aniause dismounted and reached to help her from her mare. "He's angry. And I don't blame him."

She glanced at him ruefully. "I know. But, I think Javier's mostly angry with himself. I tell you, he's hiding something."

"I'll see what I can discover."

"Speaking of angry, did you notice the strain between Baldric and his brother?"

"I did."

"I remember they were always a bit aloof with each other, but this is much worse. What do you suppose caused that?"

He hesitated, then said, "You should have seen the look Balteus gave when his brother rode away. I think this is more than brotherly strife."

"Politics?"

"It would make sense. Though Baldric advocates giving the dragon to the griffins, it's to save our people. He's very passionate about that."

"Balteus intended Elis to invade. We know that."
Destante shrugged.

"It's a fine line."

"But a gulf between them. There has to be more to
Balteus's stance."

"Do you think he plans on helping Elis with
troops?"

"I got that impression, but frankly, I don't care.
He's going to be removed from a position where he can
do harm."

"And Baldric?" Aniause shook his head.

"Time will tell, I guess. He's the elder of the two by
only a few minutes. Can you imagine, if it had been
Balteus at the coronation and I hadn't arrived when I
did?"

"I shudder at the thought. But that leads to another
question."

"Yes. Why didn't Balteus kill his brother to gain
the throne for himself?" She hesitated and softly said,
"Suppose you tell me the real reason you don't want to
be with me?"

Aniause took a step back, dark clouds in his eyes.
But then he shrugged and said, "You've already been
killed for the throne. Sooner or later, someone will try
again if there's no other way. And it will be a
permanent death. I nearly came undone when I thought
it had happened last time. I won't be able to take it if it
happens again. I can't lose you. The kingdom can't lose
you. Not at this juncture. Not ever, for me. The
possibility of marriage, or some relation like your sister
had, diminishes the chance of assassination." With that,
he turned and walked away.

She watched him go. Was that why her sister had
never married? To spare Destante the pain of losing
her? Well, it hadn't worked.

# CHAPTER 30

Aniause urged his mount through the knot of Destante's group to the far front with Javier. The guard met him with a black stare, but when Aniause said nothing, he turned face forward again, posture relaxing.

Aniause wanted some time and space so no one would interfere. They rode silently until they passed a curve in the path that hid them from the group behind. Then he quietly asked, "Who were those men?"

Javier shrugged, eyes still on the trail. "*Bandidos*."

"They seemed to know you."

"No. You are *confudido*."

Aniause shook his head. "I'm not confused. I heard them speak your name."

Javier faced him with a vicious sneer. "I'm from *aquí*, here. Everyone knows me."

The guard was well trained and brave with a blade. On the other hand, Aniause, though a physician by trade, had fought in nearly a hundred battles. Without a moment's hesitation, he lunged at Javier, punched him square in the temple, and knocked him to the ground. Pulling his sword, he jumped from his horse, and placed the point of his sword against Javier's throat before the bodyguard could scramble to his feet.

Aniause said, "You will tell me what I want to know or you'll die right here on this trail."

With a sigh, the guard settled back onto the ground. He slowly nodded.

Destante's group rounded the bend in the trail and passed them without a single glance, as if it were every day that Aniause threatened a man's life. Even Baldric kept his gaze averted, though Aniause did note a smile.

Aniause didn't think Javier was a traitor – he didn't know anything about shapeshifters – but Destante was right, the guard was hiding something. "Are you a spy for Elis? How do those men know you?"

"I told you the truth. They are *bandidos*. I know them because I was in King Elis's jail with them."

Considering how quickly the guard had come to be in their own jail, Aniause wasn't surprised. "You were a bandit. How did you get out? Did Elis cut you a deal if you would be a spy?"

"I was no *bandido*. The king's jails are always too full. I was released after a short time to make room for a murderer. I am also no spy."

"And your crime?"

Javier gave a wry grimace. "A woman. Always a woman."

Aniause relaxed his sword and motioned the man to get to his feet. "You have a choice. Either you tell the queen, or I will."

The guard nodded. "I like this job very much. I wish to keep it. I will tell her."

# CHAPTER 31

"Lord Sharoth. Lady." Destante pulled up her mare. Lord Sharoth was a tall lean man, shifting his eyes to and fro over the group. His wife was dark haired and dark eyed. A beauty at any age. Their villa was modest, small even. It also flew Elis's flag among the others.

Sharoth reached for her horse's reins. "Greetings, My Queen. News of your visit has preceded you. We have prepared a feast."

"My men and I are tired from this journey. I would like to rest for a few hours before we eat."

"Certainly, My Queen. I anticipated that and have accommodations as well as baths prepared already."

"Thank you. A hot bath is greatly appreciated." Destante smiled at his hospitality. "If it is no inconvenience to you or your staff, perhaps we will stay here a day or two."

Sharoth hesitated, and then said, "While it is a great honor, and certainly no inconvenience, I must remind you how close you are to Elis's border. If he learns of your proximity, he may decide to attack. You have made your gesture of non-fear. And I will honor you with a feast and rest, but then you must leave. For your sake, and the sake of your people. I do not think he will accept another alliance from one of our Queens."

"You take a great risk by talking to me like this." Yet another person who believed the only way a Queen could rule was on her back. Anger boiled inside her, and she was sure it could be seen in her eyes.

He dropped to one knee in front of her. "Forgive me, My Queen. It is only that I care for your safety and that of your people."

Destante stared out at the distant trees, calming her temper. He was right about Elis, though. It would be foolhardy to stay, and certain death to be caught by him. She really wanted to trust Sharoth; she needed allies. But was he on her side? He could be a dangerous man if he wasn't true.

Temper still burned in her ears, but she marshaled it under her control. She waited until her fury turned to just a simmer. "You may stand, Lord Sharoth. I find your recommendations sound and will ride on to Lord Torag's villa as soon as possible. But first, I and my men will accept your hospitality. Provided you feel there will be no repercussions on you."

He stood and carefully smiled. "I think there will not be. Elis IS cruel, but he is also smart. He most likely will not move if you do not stay. I think, in honesty, he will not attack unless he sees there is no other way to achieve his objective."

Destante turned toward the villa. "You were not in the council meeting, nor the coronation. What do you think of Noll and Elis forming a treaty?"

"It will be the end of this kingdom. Noll cannot be

swayed from his hatred of dragonkind. They killed his entire family."

"We've all lost our families to this war. Why haven't they signed the treaty yet?" She stopped and swiftly turned to look at him. "They HAVEN'T signed it yet, have they?"

"My information says they haven't. I believe they are waiting to see if you will hand over the dragon without bloodshed. Noll does not like his cousin. I think he will seek ANY other way than the treaty."

An assigned handmaid led her to her rooms. When she entered, she saw the bath in the middle of the room, steaming. On the chest by the window, Baldric's promised maps and papers waited.

She sighed. Research would have to wait until later. It took her no time to undress and slip into the bath. Her aching muscles needed this badly. As she relaxed, she nodded off. Once, she woke when she slipped down into the water and inhaled a giant noseful. She came up and out of the water coughing and sputtering. She dried off and dressed, finishing just in time for the handmaid to escort her into the dining hall.

The meal, though a feast in its own right, was nowhere near the spread Balteus had presented. Instead of platters with heaped food in the center of the table, individual eating plates and bowls were brought from the kitchen. The food itself was well cooked, but made from local ingredients with no exotic dishes. Adequate portions were served, though many were fillers: beans, rice, potatoes.

Destante glanced up at Sharoth, who was busy conversing with his wife. Both were well fed, but not excessively. She looked at the servants. None were fat, and none had a self-righteous look in their eyes. Even the dogs under the table were few, and merely well fleshed, not obese. Sharoth's money was being spent elsewhere.

There was one easy way to see where they held their allegiances.

As they finished eating, she said, "Lord Sharoth, forgive me, but I have a request of you."

He stood. "Anything, My Queen. It is all yours." He swept his hand to indicate his whole villa, his many servants, his food, and every stone in the building.

"I need a handmaiden for this trip. None of mine ride horses, and I have as yet to run into one who does. Do you have any? I would like one who is new to your staff, someone you don't depend heavily upon yet."

He glanced at his wife. "This is really my Lady's area, not mine."

The Lady smiled tightly at Destante, as the Lord sat again. She didn't seem to be quite as open to a new ruler as her husband. "Of course, My Queen. I have just recently taken on several young ladies. None of them are trained well yet. I think you'd prefer one of my older servants."

"No, I wouldn't. A new one to you will be best, actually. I prefer one who has no habits already. One who can start fresh for me. Can you bring in all candidates?"

The Lady raised her head, summoning a servant. "Bring me all the new young maidens."

By the time the meal was over, a row of seven girls was standing before Destante. It seemed to be an excessive amount of new servants needed for such a small holding, unless he was taking them in as a means of supporting and protecting them.

All seven girls were young, with fresh faces. While not as well fed as the house servants, these girls all suffered no malnutrition. They all looked upon the

Lady with something akin to love and admiration. They looked at Destante with fear. Being new to the villa, they would represent all the people within Sharoth's region. It seemed he treated his subjects well.

Destante stood and walked in front of them. She stopped in front of a firl with hair as red as Destante's own. "Do you ride a horse?"

The girl dropped her gaze to the floor.

When the girl didn't answer, Destante turned to Lady Sharoth. "She seems to have forgotten what a horse is."

The Lady rushed forward. "Consuela, do you ride a horse?"

"A bit, My Lady." She spoke softly and raised a worried gaze.

Lady Sharoth turned to Destante. "My apologies, My Queen. She's new and doesn't know what is required of them in manners. Please take one of my older servants." She lifted her arm to beckon one to her side.

Destante shook her head. "No, Lady Sharoth, I think I like this one. Consuela, if you have any family close by, run and bid them farewell. You only have a few minutes. Javier, send one of your men to accompany her, in case she forgets to return. Then have her returned to my rooms, unharmed." She glared at Javier with this last, satisfied to see a flush creep up his neck.

CHAPTER 32

Destante pivoted and walked into the kitchen. All the servants stopped and stared at her, fear etched on their faces. Then, as one, their focus shifted to behind her, as if seeking reassurance from the person who had followed. They relaxed and returned to their work. That could only mean either Sharoth or his wife had followed her, as she'd hoped.

She reached the larder and stepped inside. The food was basic, with no imports or exotic foods. What was he spending his money on? Could she trust him?

Sharoth's constrained voice came from behind her. "Does my kitchen meet with your approval?"

She turned toward him to see a dark scowl on his face. She said softly, "Please send your servants away, I must speak with you privately."

He hesitated, "There are better places to speak, My Queen."

"Yes, but if I were a spy, I would never suspect the larder as a private meeting room."

The fire left his eyes as he seemed to understand. He turned to the kitchen, "Leave these rooms. All of you await me in the anteroom." When the room emptied, he turned back to her.

She began. "I find in you an honest man who cares for his people. As I care for mine. Aniause said I could trust you. Was he right? Can I?"

Sharoth's face flushed, and he hesitated.

After a minute of not speaking, Destante smiled grimly. It appeared Aniause had been wrong. "Your lack of answer tells me all I need. Now, I only ask that you keep this conversation quiet until I return to my villa. If I learn that you do not, I will find a way to give you up to Elis, whom I'm sure will be happy to have you."

She stepped past him.

He whirled and shot out his hand, cuffing her arm, stopping her. "Forgive me, My Queen. I was overcome with emotion. I am alone here, caught between Balteus and Torag, and Elis. I'm surrounded by men with evil intent. If word gets out that I am not just as self-serving as they, it will be the end of me. My people will fall to one of them. I can't allow that to happen."

He suddenly released her arm, as if noticing for the first time that he'd actually accosted her. He dropped to his knees with his head bowed. "Forgive my familiarity, My Queen."

"Rise, Lord Sharoth. It was a minor thing. As for the matter of which we were speaking, I understand. I also have the same concerns. I won't betray you, but there are some riding with me that will."

He rose to his feet and nodded. "Lord Baldric."

"Yes, but I think there may be more. Javier for one. Uzdal vouches for his men, but I honestly don't know them. It's best we keep them all out of this. You may trust me. Also Aniause. Beyond that…." She shook her head.

"For my part, you may trust myself and Lady Sharoth. This is a dangerous line we walk here. I think most will stay with me, but fear is the ruling force in this region."

She nodded. "I see that. Time is against us at the moment. I ask that you do nothing but continue as you have. And feed me information as you can."

"I can give you men for your army. I have been surreptitiously building my troops for some time now."

"I'll count on it, when the time is right. For now, I'll take a few to add to my party."

"IF anyone asks, I will say that you demanded my men from me to guard you. It would help, if you would take some of Balteus's and Torag's men as well."

"Well thought. In fact, I will take men from every Lord's army." She looked toward the kitchen.

"My Queen," he bowed low. "My allegiance is yours."

"Thank you, Lord Sharoth."

Destante and Lord Sharoth returned to the dining hall, where his wife looked at him with raised eyebrows. He patted her hand for reassurance.

Destante excused herself and, by the time she returned to her rooms, it was all she could do to stumble through the door and fall upon her bed. She was beyond exhausted. And her body ached in every part she had, and some she didn't know she did.

She sighed. Those maps would just have to wait until tomorrow. They were safe for the night. She let herself fall asleep in her clothes.

## CHAPTER 33

Elis, as griffin, flew through the night, high above the trees. Though not one of the highest fliers in the shapeshifter world, griffins flew high enough to catch the cool breezes that flowed in currents above the lower mountains. The very tallest peaks were beyond his reach. And that was fine with him. Everything he needed and wanted was below him.

The eagle sight of the griffin noted a pinprick of light that showed through the trees, marking his destination. He dropped through the dark, landed by the campfire, and shifted to man. Ignoring his son, he wrapped the blanket offered by Cardenas around his waist. "What's the news that couldn't wait?"

Cardenas answered, "We went to her home. Clearly threatened her. Then we find her touring her kingdom as if we'd never spoken. She's obviously not afraid. So, I followed through on our warning. Set a band of my boys to attack her, to send her scurrying for shelter. Instead, she joined in the fight herself, neatly dispatching two of my men. And Sire?”

Elis had been staring into the fire, listening. Now he turned his full attention on Cardenas.

“Javier was with her as master of her guard.”

The griffin king pursed his lips. Javier. He didn’t see how it could present a problem, but it probably would. Such was the nature of Javier. When would he be rid of that man? “Where are they now?”

“Directly across the river from here.”

“Sharoth.” So close.

Cardenas nodded and they both fell silent while Elis thought out the possible options and repercussions. He shook off one plan after another. Finally, he spoke. “It changes nothing. Though some of the other shapeshifter clans will naturally side with her, we can’t risk more joining her because of an unprovoked attack. Stay close and watch what she does. We still don’t know who the dragon is.”

“If we kill them all, what does it matter?”

“It will matter if the dragon isn’t on this trip with them and he survives.”

Cardenas nodded his understanding, and, still without a word to his own son, Elis once again shifted to griffin and flew back to his castle. One thing was certain: Destante was obviously not her sister.

CHAPTER 34

The first thing in the morning, Aniause was awakened by a servant requesting him for an audience with Destante. A memory sprang forward of another time, hundreds of years ago, being awakened for an audience with Destante and the new queen, her sister Delcinae.

The night before had been full of revelry, such as the custom was upon the death of a dignitary, in this case, the king. Aniause's head was thick with mead and his whole body smelled of smoke from a funeral pyre.

He'd moved slow getting ready for his meeting, and when he arrived, he found only Destante waiting for him.

She'd looked on him with a mix of sorrow and amusement. "Pack your doctor things. Our new queen has managed to procure you passage to the Orient so you can study their medical techniques."

"So quickly?" He blinked hard. He'd only mentioned it in passing a few days ago as they'd prepared the King's body.

Destante nodded. "It's an opportune time. We are also leaving Spain, though not for the Orient. We're moving our clan to Mexico where we can live in peace."

He shook his head. "There will never be peace as long as the dragon lives."

"I fear you're right. But you still need to go. Don't mince your studies. Hurry back to join us; I'll miss you."

He'd left within the hour.

And now, Aniause was yawning and moving slow again, stumbling across the floor to the wash basin to cleanse himself.

By the time he arrived at Destante's assigned rooms, she was chomping at the bit like a horse held at the start of a race for too long.

She asked, "Did I wake you?"

"In fact, you did." He motioned toward the maps and books on the bed. "Is that why you wanted to see me?"

"In a bit, yes. First, let's walk, you and I; we're to meet Sharoth and Javier. Though I can't trust my bodyguard, I can still use him." She led the way through the door, saying nothing until they reached the extensive gardens that Lady Sharoth personally tended.

She placed a hand on his arm and stopped. "No one else has arrived yet, but I can begin. I think I've hit on a way to recruit for our army without Noll and Elis deciding to attack early."

Aniause spoke through a stifled yawn. "And what is that?"

"Most of the guards will need to stay with the lords along the borders, but we will also recruit for guards on my journey. Then, send them on during the night to join our forces at home and other key places."

"Someone is bound to notice our guard retinue doesn't grow."

"Only if they follow us. I'll take some from each lord. Those are the ones we'll send on. I believe we can keep the exact number hidden."

"If Balteus and Torag are any indication, there will be quite a few who have chosen to ally with Elis and Noll to be spared the affects of the battle. Are you going to dispose of them?"

"Most certainly, but not until we're ready to deal with the griffins themselves. Everything, and I mean everything, must be kept secret. It must look like I'm still trying to decide what course of action to take, like I'm polling the phoenix lords. No doubt word has gotten back that I've learned of the possible alliance. However, both Noll and Elis, hating each other, will wait to see what I do."

She leaned in to a fragrant rose, inhaling deeply. Aniause's heart squeezed tight against his ribs. He longed to pull her to him, right then, and kiss her until neither of them had any more breath.

Destante, as if knowing his desires, looked at him with heartbreak naked in her eyes. When he took a step back from her, she smiled sadly.

He cleared his throat and then said, "I'm glad you've taken Sharoth as an ally. I had hoped it would be so. I'm curious though, why you took a handmaid from his court, particularly when you told me you didn't want one."

"Seeing them all helped me decide the kind of man he is. Did you notice that most of Balteus's and Torag's servants are frightened of them? Not so with Sharoth's. Further, the girl, Consuela, can always act as messenger for us."

"If she doesn't run away. She looks frightened."

"She'll settle in, when she sees I won't hurt her."

"I also didn't fail to notice that she is tall and red-haired like you."

Destante's eyes twinkled, but when she opened her mouth to speak, she snapped it shut again. Aniause turned to see Sharoth approaching.

The lord bowed low. "I trust all is to your satisfaction?"

"Indeed it is. You have been most generous."

"I have been telling Aniause about the men you'll be adding to my guard."

"I am happy to serve in any way I can." Again, he bowed low. "Anything you desire is yours. I am but a servant for you."

Spying Javier coming toward them she said, "And now, I'll tell you why I asked to meet with all of you. I intend to go sneak into Elis's home."

For a split-second there was silence. Sharoth's face blanched. Javier's turned fire red. Aniause just stared at her. Then, they all spoke at once, shaking their heads and gesticulating.

"I'm not letting you go!"

"You'll endanger your people!"

"It's too *peligroso* — dangerous!"

She held up her hand until they silenced. Then she began again. "I misspoke. Let me rephrase myself. I need you three to work with me to find a way that I can sneak into Elis's home safely and return just as safely."

They stared at her. It was Aniause who eventually broke the silence. "I remember you sneaking around in Spain, dressed as a man."

She nodded. "I can certainly do that again."

Javier shook his head. "*Es imposible.* You'll be seen for a woman."

"Really? Care to place a bet on that? No one discovered me then, I doubt anyone will discover me now."

Uncertainty clouded his brow and he fell silent again.

She turned to Sharoth. "We'll leave from another location to protect you and your people."

He nodded hesitantly, color returning to his face. "That would be best, My Queen. It's not that I fear fighting Elis, but we're not ready for battle."

"No, we're not. But he sent men into my own home to show me I'm not safe from him. I intend to return the favor. I intend to show him a bigger gesture of non-fear."

Aniause spoke up again. His voice was soft. "If he killed your sister, as we believe, then he has discovered how a phoenix CAN be killed."

"Then, we'll have to make sure he doesn't succeed again." Destante and the three men spent most of the morning pouring over the maps, picking out the best route to and from Elis's home. It was decided she and Javier would leave from Torag's European-style castle to alleviate any suspicion of Sharoth. By late afternoon, Destante and her party rode on. Torag's wasn't far; they could easily reach it by nightfall.

## CHAPTER 35

Javier rode behind the phoenix queen, deep in his thoughts after the meeting with Lord Sharoth. They rode hard, and the trail was clear and easy, though Colima promised it wouldn't be for much longer. Gases hissed from vents in the ground. The earth trembled beneath their horses' feet.

"You're very quiet," Destante said, turning fully in her saddle to face him. Far ahead, *el doctor* rode with Baldric, deep in discussion. The other two guards scouted even further ahead.

He sighed deeply. "There is something I must tell you."

"And you don't think I'll like it?"

"I think you will misunderstand."

"Tell me. I promise to keep an open mind."

He sighed again, nudging his horse beside her. Likely he was cutting his throat. "My mother was *servienta* in King Noll's castle. I grew up there."

"It didn't escape my attention how well you speak English."

He nodded. "When I was old enough, several of us were sent to King Elis. Eventually I became a guard in the king's court. I was caught with his mistress and jailed."

"Are you working for him still? Are you his spy?"

He felt her eyes on him, boring into his heart to see any lies he might have told. He choked on that look, not drawing a single breath. He didn't dare to look up, to meet her gaze. Slowly, his breathing returned again. He said, "I am not a spy, but I have seen many things in Elis's employ. I can tell you there is more than one man working for him."

After a long moment, she said, "I believe you. Do you know Noll's castle well also?"

CHAPTER 36

It was nearing dusk when Destante and her retinue arrived. From the exterior, it seemed Torag was no better than Balteus. He also had a castle, after the European fashion, but it was huge, much larger than many in Spain, even. Multiple tall turrets sported many flags, including Elis's. It only lacked a moat.

Destante slipped to the ground. Torag didn't meet them in front of his castle wall as the other lords had. What was his game? She handed off the horses to Javier and entered, where she found Torag waiting for her in the front chamber. "My Queen. I trust your journey has been going well?"

"Yes. Thank you. Though, we're not as welcome some places as others."

Torag took on a distant look. "Ah yes. Lord Sharoth."

"We seek your accommodations for two or three nights. Will that be possible?" Of course, she knew it would be, she was queen after all.

"Indeed." He moved close to her and let his gaze rove over her face. "I shall be happy to have you."

Have her? What did he mean by that? Was he flirting with her? Destante paused. Had her sister had more than one lover? She couldn't imagine them together, but then again, she couldn't imagine her sister with Elis either. Until she knew more, she'd be wise to play along. "Lord Torag, we are surrounded by your people. Your own wife is somewhere within this building. Walls DO speak."

She pulled away and motioned down a passage toward what she assumed would be her rooms. Was Torag the man who betrayed them? "I'm tired now and would like to rest before our meal. My room is this way?"

Torag smiled knowingly.

When they reached her door, she offered her hand to him. He hesitated, and he leaned low to kiss it, caressing her palm with his thumb at the same time. When he stood, his eyes were full of meaning.

She turned into her room, shutting the door behind her. Almost immediately, someone knocked at the door. Thinking it was Torag again, she only opened the door enough to look out. She wanted to give him no opportunity to get into her room, though she could handle him if he did.

Javier's face appeared on the other side of the door opening. Relief swept through her, and she pulled the door open wide. After he strode in, and she shut the door, she asked, "You saw?"

He hesitated, and then he gave a short jerk of his head in affirmation. "If he intends a midnight visit, he'll discover we're gone."

"We'll have to postpone our secret trip by one night then. And you will have to stand guard tonight from the inside of the door. Post another on the outside."

"It will be a pleasure to have a surprise ready for him when he arrives tonight. I will, however, stand there." He pointed to the terrace door. "If Torag is the man I think he is, he won't seek to come in the front door, but rather sneak in through the window or a hidden passage."

Destante frowned. "I'm not sure I can sleep with you standing there." She was no prude, but a man who wasn't her lover standing that close?

He shrugged. "I can sing you to sleep, if you like. I have a fine voice."

She stared at the earnestness on his face and laughed. "No, I think that will be quite all right. I'll get used to you there."

At the evening meal, Torag kept his attentions on Destante. Looking at the faces at the table, she could see it was not lost on any in the room, including his wife, who would not look their direction.  It was obvious the Lady had been faced with Torag's wandering passions before. Aniause did his best to engage the lord in conversation, and pull his attention away from Destante. However, it only seemed to make the lord more impatient.

Torag eventually said, as he was lifting a cup of wine to his lips, "I heard about the skirmish … yesterday, was it? You actually joined the fight."

Destante paused in her eating, soup still pooled in her spoon, and looked up at him. "It was brought near enough to put me in danger. I had little choice."

He stared at her, with a smile playing on his face. "I was told that, in fact, you dispatched two men all by yourself."

"That is greatly exaggerated, Lord Torag. I merely pushed them to fall forward where another man cut off their heads. It was just luck."

"Indeed." He looked her up and down, and then took a drink from his wine. "I should have liked to have seen that."

Aniause spoke up. "One more sword would have given us greater ease of mind regarding the queen's safety."

"I'm sure your guard had it well under control." He eyed Javier, who stood along the wall of the room, behind Destante's seat.

She smiled and returned to her food. In truth, she was no longer hungry. She stood. "Now I wish you a good night. Please don't stand."

Everyone stood anyway. Lord Torag said, "My Queen, you have left much of your food untouched. Is there fault with our meal?"

She shook her head. "It's only that I get very tired on this journey. I never sleep well and so am awake far ahead of the rest of everyone. So I also go to sleep ahead of the rest. In truth, I prefer it this way. It enables me to get many thoughts straight in my head before the day begins. Good night."

She turned and left, with Javier following. Once in her room, she slipped into bed, fully dressed. Javier took his station by the terrace door. She said, "I don't know how I'll sleep, knowing an uninvited guest will most probably visit during the night."

Javier began to hum a melody. He did indeed have a nice voice. She began to relax, and then she felt the heaviness of sleep come and let herself fall into it.

It was the sound of whispering that awakened her. By the door stood two shadows. She recognized the voice as Javier's.

"—any man, no matter what station, to sneak into the queen's room in the middle of the night. By the laws of this kingdom, I could kill you right here, right now, even within your own walls.”

Torag's voice answered. “And what are you doing here, in her private sleeping chamber?”

“I'm only here to protect her from you.”

“I wonder how well you will protect her from yourself. Let go of me, I’ll leave as quietly as I came.”

The two shadows separated and one moved out the door, into the moonlight. The other shadow came close to the bed. “He won’t return. You can go back to sleep now.”

As he started to walk away, toward the door between the two rooms, she said, “Javier, thank you.”

CHAPTER 37

Throughout the following day, Aniause followed Destante and the rest of the queen's party as Torag eagerly showed off his holdings. His stables, in particular, were worthy of admiration.

The horses were neither too fat, nor too thin, but well exercised and properly fed. Their coats gleamed as if polished metal.

Aniause had to admit he'd never seen such impressive horseflesh.

"The key," The Lord of the castle said, "is repetition within a strict schedule. If any of my horses are groomed late, the responsible party is flogged. I won't tolerate even the smallest delay."

He led the way to a black mare that glistened like night on a lake. "This, My Queen, is for you. She is in foal to my stud, there."

He gestured to the end stall where a blood red stallion paced. The leer on Torag's face was unmistakable, as was the unspoken suggestion of taking

Destante as his mistress.

Destante flushed. "Lord Torag, she's the most beautiful mare I've ever seen, but I have much riding to do yet." She cupped the mare's muzzle between her hands and whispered words too soft for anyone else to hear.

"She'll be fine as long as you don't take her into too rough territory or tax her too much. I'll give your guard," he nodded toward Javier, "instructions on how to care for her."

"I will care for her myself."

Aniause's heart pulled at the adoration he saw pouring out of Destante onto the horse. How he longed to be held in her hands in that way! To be looked at like that once more! He dropped his gaze to the floor before he came undone.

He felt a hand clamp on his shoulder and looked up to see Baldric watching him. Not a word passed between them, but Aniause felt a small amount of comfort. It didn't surprise him that Baldric knew of the past relationship he'd had with the queen. The whole kingdom knew. What surprised him was the compassion. He nodded and he and Baldric moved on, following Destante and Torag as they left the stable.

As the rest of the day progressed, he watched Destante's eyes fold into tighter and tighter slits, and her jaw clench more and more. By the time the evening repast was ready, she excused herself because of a headache.

Dutifully, Aniause rose and detoured by his room to pick up medical supplies. When he reached Destante's room, he found her lying on her bed, arm slung over her eyes. Walking to the window, he pulled the drapes shut. He then went to a small table by the bed and mixed a remedy. "While I realize our plan was

134

for you to withdraw early from the meal with the excuse of a headache, I believe this is real."

When she spoke, her words were slurred and her voice was soft. "It is. How can anything hurt this much?"

He held out the bottle of mixed ingredients to her. "Drink. This will help."

Slowly she raised herself, wincing. She reached for the bottle and swallowed the remedy in one swift gulp.

As she lowered to her pillow again, he carefully said, "You know, you don't need to go tonight."

"I've already put it off by one night. If I don't go now, something else may make me put it off again."

"Would that be such a bad thing? I don't think this is a wise course of action."

She looked at him thoughtfully. "I know. It probably isn't, but I refuse to be intimidated and insulted. I'm going, and that's final. Consuela knows what to do?"

"She does. And now I see why you have her."

"Many reasons, including the ones I originally told you. It amazes me the amount of things I can think of to do with that girl. She can be my double, a courier, a spy, and all kinds of other things."

"If you can trust her."

"It's your job to make sure we can."

CHAPTER 38

In the dark of that night, Destante woke at Javier standing at the entrance of her room, softly calling her name.

She said, "I guess I fell asleep. I'll be ready in a moment."

"I'll wait in the hall." He withdrew, pulling the door shut behind him.

Once dressed in her merchant's disguise, she called him to rejoin her. When he entered, his eyes widened and he looked her up and down. Slowly, he nodded. "You just may pass."

With a deep smile at his understatement, she led the way across the terrace, down the hill, and to the stable. Once there, she said, "Thank you again for stopping Torag last night."

He nodded. "I don't think he'll cause you any more trouble. Still, it's not too late to cancel our visit to Elis."

She glared at him. "We're going."

At the stable, Destante looked longingly at the

black mare Torag had gifted her. But the horse was too flashy. Instead, she rode one of the guard's horses, something any merchant would ride: tall, gangly, and with a back more swayed than any peasants house.

She and Javier headed east, riding from town to town and skirting the edge of Elis's river border far enough inland to not be noticed. Once they'd gone far enough, they crossed the water at a wide delta onto Elis's property, passing the gagging stench of piked heads.

Shortly after sunrise, they rode through one of the side gates of the enormous wall Elis had erected to protect what was his. Elis's family had moved to Mexico only a few years after Destante's had, following because of the rumor of a dragon. They carried with them the European tradition of city architecture as well as the materials to begin building. Halfway up the side of the city walls was a clear demarcation of where the paler old world materials had run out and they had switched to darker local fabrications.

Entrusting their horses to an inn near the gate, they entered streets teeming with people. Myriads of color and motion flowed everywhere Destante looked. Hawkers cried out their wares from overburdened tables. Hot cinnamon mixed with the scent of ale and flowers. Religious bells attached to long robes tinkled as acolytes passed with massive throngs of volcano-panicked people.

Javier turned to her, and his face seemed to magically regress in age. His eyes filled with mischievousness. He smiled and took her hand, pulling her through the mass of people, shouting over his shoulder. "The best way to get into Elis's palace is this way."

"You might not want to hold a merchant's hand." She looked pointedly at him. "Nor a queen's, for that matter."

Self-consciously, he nodded and dropped his grip. "You'll have to stay close."

Then they were off again, twisting through the currents of the morning crowd. Once, a giant of a man stepped between them and the throng swept Destante away. Try as she might to move out of its eddy, she couldn't.

All at once, Javier was beside her again. He cuffed her arm, pushing and pulling her in the direction he wished to go.

Then, they were out of the crowd and in a tiny, dark alley that passed under the inner wall, near the palace. Javier let go of her and stepped through a black doorway. Destante slowly followed, brushing her fingertips on the wall as she traipsed behind him through twists and turns. The ground had a gradual upslope to it. Light crept into the tunnel and traces of worn brick showed beneath her feet. They reached a set of stairs and started climbing.

It wasn't far up the staircase before Javier stopped in an alcove. He leaned against the wall, listening. With a nod to her, he shoved his shoulder against the stone and pushed. The wall swung silently outwards to reveal a room of magnificent size. He turned to her and pulled her close, whispering, "This is a mistress's room. She would be in the court with Elis right now."

Destante remembered the story he'd told her and hoped he hadn't lied when he'd said he wouldn't betray her. Sneaking into Elis's castle would be the worst place to be caught. "I'm surprised he kept her."

"He has many mistresses. The one caught with me was beheaded," he said sadly. He led her out of the room and into the hallway. Standing up tall, he strode down the center of the passage a step ahead of her. Just before they reached the main court, he took a turn to the left into another, smaller passage. If she understood the layout of this court, then he was leading her to stand near the throne. He stopped near a drape and pulled it aside to reveal a little alcove. As she entered, he pressed his finger to his lips and moved next to her.

An arrogant voice on the other side of the drape spoke. It was a voice Destante knew: Alejandro Luis Cardenas. "Your son promised the villagers –"

A stronger, yet softer voice broke in. "I don't care what he's promised. Are my soldiers in place?"

"Since dawn, My Liege."

The throne groaned, and the voice came from a different position now. "Fine, let them have the village then. If the people there want to hide a known felon, then they will pay the consequences."

As it spoke, the voice crossed the room. "I'm tired of my son giving in to his people's demands. He will learn, albeit the hard way, that to rule, one must have a firm hand and be willing to crush rebellions before they arise." Judging from the echo off the wall in the opposite direction, the last words were spoken from outside the room.

"Yes, My King." Cardenas's voice followed the other out of the room.

Javier led her back the way they came. As they walked down the main hallway, a door burst open, and a small knot of men entered the passage, heading toward them. Cardenas walked beside a man in the center of the group, who was very tall, close to seven feet. He had dark hair and equally dark eyes that shifted back and forth between Destante and Javier. As the men approached, he stared at Javier and then he flicked his gaze over her, looking her up and down.

He frowned.

Javier didn't waiver, except to step to the side, bowing his head in obedience. This, then, must be Elis. Destante had seen him once, when they were young and still in Spain. He'd changed, yet there were still remnants of the young man she remembered. She stepped smartly beside Javier and bowed as well. The group passed, and she tipped her head to watch them continue down the hall.

She felt a nudge and turned to see Javier once again moving down the corridor toward the mistress's bed chamber. She hurried beside him and whispered. "We should go back and listen more."

He shook his head. "He recognized me. But I don't think he knew you. It's just a matter of seconds before he sends someone to apprehend me. We need to hurry."

They rushed to the secret door. Then down the stairs and through the tunnel to the alley. "Are you saying Elis doesn't know about that secret entry?"

Javier shrugged. "I'm sure he does, but there are so many, he would have to guess which one we used. Forgive me, but we'll have to get through the crowd quickly." He slid an arm around her waist, holding her bicep with his other hand, as they reached the crowd and melded in with it. He seemed to pick her up and move her in the way he wanted her to go, and in no time they were through the flood of people and into another alley on the other side.

He looked down at her, and removed his arm from around her waist. "Forgive my familiarity. I meant nothing by it. It was the best way to get us across the street." He bowed, waiting for her reaction.

She could have been furious. Should have been. But the laughter at his antics that had started building since he told her about his misfortune with Elis boiled out of her. And it *had* been fun being carried across the street like that. With a failure at a straight face, she said. "Well, I'm glad you did. I would have been swept away."

He returned her grin with one of his own, then led the way to the stable where they fetched their horses, broke into a gallop, and headed back toward the border. When they finally slowed to a walk again, she asked, "Tell me about Elis's son."

"Elis thinks he's a bleeding heart. The two of them have been at odds all their lives."

"Elis seems very authoritarian. A tyrant, almost."

Javier nodded. "He is. He squelches anyone who doesn't agree with his policies. His prisons are always full."

"If he takes over our kingdom, what can we expect?"

"I don't know for sure. He hasn't acquired any new properties since I've been watching him. I would imagine he will remove all the lords form their regions and replace them with those of his choosing. He will probably institute a martial law, and raise the taxes evenly throughout his whole kingdom. The lords will loose their free choice to rule."

"And he'll place his son as overlord, no doubt. What will he do with me?"

Javier's face flamed. "He will probably take you to his bed, and then throw you in prison."

CHAPTER 39

Aniause scrutinized the imposter queen. He'd sat her in the shadows where it was difficult to see any distinct facial features. Furthermore, he'd had her dressed in a shapeless robe to hide her form. Destante was more ample in certain areas than Consuela.

He'd styled her hair like the queen's too. As a final touch, he'd had her slouch in a chair, such as an ill person might do. He walked around the room, trying to see her from any and all possible angles that Lord Torag might use. All-in-all, if no one came too close, the subterfuge should work. It would be his job to make sure everyone kept their distance.

A tear slid down Consuela's cheek and her lower lip quivered. She pressed her eyes tightly shut.

Aniause rushed to her. Poor girl. This was a hard thing he was asking: to impersonate a queen. If they were caught, it could mean death, even though sanctioned by the queen, herself. "Don't be afraid. If you do as I told you, no one will suspect a thing. Please trust me."

She opened her eyes. "Yes, Sir. What should I do if I'm found out?"

"Nothing. I'll take care of it. I'll be right here with you. Now, practice what I taught you."

"I feel ill and require solitude for the day. Please leave," she recited, her voice lower and softer than her normal. The girl's fear thickened the words, adding a ragged edge to the command. Such as an ill queen might sound.

Aniause smiled. Perfect. They were ready.

He walked to the door, opened it, and ordered the waiting chamber maid to send for the lord of the manor. The girl scurried away and Aniause returned to wait with Consuela.

They didn't have to wait long.

Within minutes a rap came on the door and Torag burst into the room. Spying the queen, he started toward her, smiling. What the lord thought was going to happen was something Aniause was thankful he'd never know. He stepped between the two, hand up, effectively stopping Torag at the predetermined place.

The lord halted, anger playing with confusion across his face, glaring at Aniause. "What is the meaning of this?"

Consuela spoke, her voice no more than a husky whisper. "Lord Torag, as you can see, I'm quite ill. I require solitude for the day."

Torag stared at her a moment, and Aniause worried he'd discovered the truth, but then the lord said, "Yes, My Queen. I trust it wasn't that you missed last evening's meal that made you ill?"

Consuela said nothing, her eyes wide with panic.

Aniause stepped into the conversation. "The queen will be fine. The headache that sent her to her room early last night is lingering. A quiet day of rest should take care of it. Her meals should be sent here." He crowded Torag.

The lord peered around Aniause and studied the imposter queen hidden in the half-shadows, disappointment clear on his face. He opened his mouth to speak, but Aniause beat him to it.

"She will no doubt be well again by morning. These things don't usually last long. However, before you leave, there is a matter about which I wish to discuss. In private, if you please, Sir." He swept his hand toward the door.

For a moment, Torag balked. He half-step toward Consuela, his eyes dark and piercing.

In that very second, Consuela's fear won out and she let out a breathy moan.

Aniause now turned to face her, and her moan caught mid-way on sudden tears as she met his gaze. She dropped her head. He pivoted back to Torag. "You see how her head hurts her. Please, Sir. Your presence is too much. You must leave."

He again crowded the lord, motioning toward the door with an outstretched hand. Torag slowly nodded, his brow wrinkled with concern. He complied.

Once out in the hall, Aniause ushered him to a quiet alcove. "Forgive me, Sir. I have no other pressing business. I didn't want to discuss this in front of the queen for fear of making her illness worse. The truth is, she has not been able to get over the loss of her sister."

Torag nodded his understanding and Aniause continued. "The queen is caught in some kind of limbo. She grieves when she believes her sister is past rebirth, but other times she is determined that Delcinae is just late returning. If she could know for sure, one way or another, I believe she could be whole again. She's strong, but as it is, she's lost in this repeating cycle of hope and grief. Even this trip through the kingdom was really in hope of finding her sister once more."

Torag was silent a moment, his gaze traveling the hallway. Then he quietly said, "Our late queen will not be reborn."

Aniause's heart chilled. "And you know this with certainty? It would mean much help for Destante."

"She will never return from the ground. I know this to be a fact."

Biting back his fury, Aniause shook the lord's hand. "Thank you. I hope that soon our new queen will be on the mend. Now, if you don't mind, I'll return to her and set her on that path."

As he entered the queen's room, his heart was battering his ribs. His temper was simmering. Either Torag, himself, had killed Delcinae. Or he had assisted Elis in her death. That much was certain.

Destante had ridden right into the mouth of the monster. He had to send help.

CHAPTER 40

Destante and Javier reached the border river long past nightfall and waded the horses across it. They were met by Baldric and his two guards. The phoenix lord's anger seemed to almost form a palpable cloud around him. He reached for her horse's reins and pulled her aside. "Aniause told me of your scheme. He sent me to protect you. And I must say, the next time you decide to gamble with your own life, please don't do it in such a foolhardy fashion. You have risked us all."

"Lord Baldric, you speak out of line, especially considering you were jailed for attempted assassination."

"I only speak of this to you, because I know you are new to your throne and aren't wise in the ways of leading."

"You speak of this because you hope to drive a wedge between us. It is your hope that with us at odds, the lords will take sides. Since they know you, though they don't like you, they will side with you rather than with a pitiful girl, whom they don't know and has no army. It is treason. Watch your steps closely."

"My Queen!" He bowed low. "I am loyal to the crown."

"To the crown yes, but only as long as you see it coming to YOUR head." She rode past him.

"You do me an injustice!"

"Do I?" She whirled her horse around and rode right up to him, her knee knocking harshly against his. She locked her gaze with his. "Do my eyes tell you I'm the fool you think I am?"

He searched her gaze. "No, My Queen. They do not."

"I'm no fool, I'm no stranger to leadership, and I'm no stranger to fighting. You may have forgotten the battles in Spain and the troops we led, but I assure you, I haven't. Make no mistake, Lord Baldric, though you are my cousin, I'm no stranger to betrayal either. I know how to deal with it."

"My Queen, I am true to the kingdom."

She studied him a minute. Everything she knew about her cousin told her this was true. From their youth, he'd always been passionate about his father's people. Would he make a good ally? "Yes, I believe you are. But it is MY kingdom. Not yours." She waited until he bowed his head, then she turned her horse and continued toward Torag's. "I wonder what you would have done, as King. Would you have turned over the dragon?"

"As a last resort, yes. Anything to save our people."

"You're aware this is the last dragon alive? When he dies, as Elis would surely kill him, their race will be extinguished."

"As I told your Aniause, my concern is for our people, lest we also become extinguished. That dragon will not live forever. Their race is already gone to the grave."

She laughed. "And you trusted Elis after he ordered you to kill your own blood cousins?"

"I didn't kill anyone. As I told Aniause."

"Keeping a phoenix from rebirth is death. Or has it been so long since you've tasted a blade that you've forgotten."

The bit of color that was coming back to his face retreated, leaving him as a ghost. He said nothing for a moment, then said, "I had nothing to do with your sister."

She scrutinized his face, looking for any trace that would give away a lie, but saw none. "Perhaps. But the fact remains, your allegiance to Elis would have failed. He would have destroyed us anyway and taken our lands for his own."

She continued. "And your brother, do you trust him to have left you alive on the throne when he's next in line? He's loyal to Elis and no one else."

Baldric gave a heavy sigh from behind her. "It's true, he wants to cede into Elis's rule. I took precautions against Balteus's attempt at my life. His court is laced with my men."

The path widened and Destante moved to the side to make room for Baldric to ride up beside her. When they were young, still in Spain, he was her favorite cousin. Many of the old court had expected them to marry, but no one knew she'd already bonded with Aniause. Except Baldric, and he took great pains to keep her secret and protect her from other would-be suitors. They often rode together in hunts. A pang of longing filled her for those days and she shook her head at herself.

When Baldric came abreast, she said, "I don't like

you. But I respect you, and I now believe you will never let this kingdom fall. I will call upon you heavily in the days to come. Together, we will stand against Noll and Elis."

"What are your plans concerning the treaty?"

"I believe the treaty will allow them to sweep across our lands and take it as their own. Elis will eventually betray Noll and take his lands as well. We are only the means to the end."

They rode in silence for some time before Baldric asked again, "What are your plans?"

"Noll and Elis are watching to see what I will do. It will buy some time to build our armies. Expect there to be spies in your ranks."

He nodded. "I have already beheaded three."

"How many Lords are loyal to you and our kingdom?"

He hesitated, but then answered. "There are seven who will fight with me."

"But will they fight Noll and Elis, or only me?"

"They will fight whomever I fight."

She turned in her saddle and looked at him. "I won't allow the day to come for us to war each other. But I won't be overrun either. As I said, together I believe we can keep our kingdom and protect the dragon. But I suspect Noll and Elis are hoping for you and I to fight. It will make their job that much easier."

"I had already thought that, My Queen."

"No doubt that's why you didn't strike at me the minute I took your crown from you."

His face reddened. "It is."

"And you were intending to strike later, if there was still a kingdom left standing."

He nodded.

"I *am* curious what you hoped to gain by burning a

phoenix."

He hesitated, then said, "Your head was not burnt separately as I had instructed. It rolled against your body as the pyre settled in the ashes. It was as simple as that."

She smiled at that. "Indeed."

Baldric fell behind her again, as the path narrowed. She said over her shoulder. "I believe that the treaty idea was formulated when it looked like you were going to take the crown. I don't imagine they intended to let you keep the land. Sooner or later they would have taken it from you. But now Elis may be waiting until you and I fight and will move on his own to take our kingdom. I think it's better we stand united, don't you?"

"Yes, My Queen." There was no hint of malice or hesitancy in his voice. Had he reconciled to her rule? Time would tell.

"I am loathe to take you away from your lands while battle is threatening so close to you, but I need you in my councils."

"I have an able Army Chief."

"Good, then I will expect you there promptly. What I heard at Elis's gave me reason to think I need to cut my tour off and return home to prepare. Send your men to notify all the lords of a meeting."

CHAPTER 41

Destante, with her group, returned to Torag's stable long after midnight. She saw Aniause was standing a little away from the stables, shoulders slumped, staring at the moon. When she dismounted, he motioned her aside. "Forgive me for sending Baldric. I learned some information that worried me for your safety. Were you able to study Elis?"

"I did. And it didn't please me to find it as I'd guessed. My plans to tour the kingdom have to be put aside. We must return home. How did it go with Consuela? Does Torag suspect anything?"

"It went exactly as you'd planned. Though, the news of your continued illness puts Torag in quite a foul mood."

He watched Baldric unsaddle his horse.

Destante followed Aniause's gaze. "Baldric and I formed a truce of sorts. We may clash again later, but for now, he has promised unity against a common foe."

"He's a tyrant, every bit as much as Noll or Elis."

"Yes, but he's OUR tyrant and I think he honestly cares about our people."

As her borrowed horse was being led away, she called Javier back to her. He handed off the reins and approached.

She said, "I have a task for you."

He frowned and opened his mouth to argue, but she held up her hand, stopping him. "Yes, it must be you, and no other. You're the only one I trust."

"It will be noticed if I'm not here."

"It can be explained. I need you to send one of your men to meet with one of Sharoth's men tonight. While it's still dark, in the woods. Give him the message that Sharoth is to beseech those to the south of us to join in the fight on our behalf. If they need to be bought, so be it. Then, I want you to ride home as fast as you can. Find the man I pointed out to you a few days ago, Miguel Angél." She told Javier what she wanted.

"Do you understand?" she asked.

"Yes, My Lady." He slowly nodded, then turned, and walked toward a short, thick shouldered fellow. Within just a few minutes, his chosen messenger mounted and rode off at a full-out gallop.

A few seconds later, Javier mounted his own horse and raced in a different direction.

She turned for the palace and her room, sleep dragging her feet. Except for a few minutes the night she and Javier had left to visit Elis, she'd been awake well over 36 hours now, and her warm comfortable bed was calling her. Aniause walked with her, the moon lighting his creased brow. He walked close and his head was tilted slightly her direction. He was worried for her and it touched her.

Still, after everything he'd said, after all the

decisions he'd made, he still cared for her. Phoenixes only had one true love, one fated mate. Aniause was hers, she'd known it since the moment they met as children. Time would never erase that, but for now, it seemed, they were destined to live their lives apart. It would take time to repeal the necessary laws that kept them separate. She was so lonely for him. The thought overburdened her and tears burned in her eyes. She shook her head violently. No tears. Not now. Not ever. This was the way it had to be. That was abundantly clear.

They entered Torag's stronghold and walked down the silent dark hallway. Low candle flames sent flickering shadows on the walls, escorting them deeper into the keep.

As they neared the private sleeping rooms, a door creaked open and Aniause pulled Destante into a recess so small they were pressed tight together. He whispered, "Torag."

She looked behind her, spotting the lord skulking down the hall and entering a chambermaid's room. Of course.

When she turned back, Aniause was staring at her, a fierce predator look glinting in his eyes. The wild animal musk of phoenix pheromones filled the confined space.

Without a word, she wound her arms around his neck, even as his hands slid behind her back and he pulled her tight against him. Her lips burned at the first touch of his and she pressed against him, her needy body molding to his. He matched her fierceness with his own, crushing her mouth with his hunger, opening it and pillaging the depths with his tongue.

The only sounds were his deep, raspy breaths and her soft moan.

Slowly he pulled away and glanced down the hallway. When he looked back at her again, his gaze was guarded, though his breathing was still ragged. He said, "I'm sorry."

"Don't." She shook her head and patted his chest. "Please don't apologize."

He nodded, took her hand, and hurried her down the hall to her room.

She turned to open her door and when she looked back, he was already walking away.

CHAPTER 42

Sleep didn't come for Aniause that night. He lay awake, staring at the ceiling, occasionally cursing the day of his birth, and replaying the kiss in his mind. What had he done?

The pheromones had clogged his brain. That had to be it.

But, she'd felt so good in his embrace.

Lately, he'd felt the same as if she'd never returned: hollow. Worse even, because he could see her, and smell her, but not touch her. And it hadn't escaped his notice that she avoided looking at him whenever she could. Even during a conversation, her gaze sought some other point to fix on.

If he was going to support her as queen the way her title demanded, he was going to have to stay away completely from her. It astounded him to admit, he was actually jealous of Javier, who was near her constantly.

The same thoughts rolled round and round in his head until he lunged to his feet and dressed. Then he stood rooted to the center of his room. He had nowhere to go. The lady of the house had no gardens for him to roam. If he stayed where he was, he would surely make a bigger mistake than the one he already had; Destante's room was just down the hall.

In a sudden decision, he strode out of his room. He'd go to the stables. Surely the quiet calm of the beasts would be better company than the thoughts in his head.

The door of the stable opened easily to him, letting a thick wave of warm horse-scent to roll over him. Despite his somber mood, he smiled. There was no other comfort like that of a horse. Wandering from stall to stall, he paused to pay his respects to each occupant.

Most were half-asleep, quietly chewing on wisps of dried grass. A couple paced along the stone walls of their stalls, nervous from the ground tremblings. There was a mare in season, who, every time Torag's red stud called, lifted her tail and softly nickered.

When he came upon the little black mare Torag had given to Destante, he couldn't help but admire the animal. She was a fine horse. The volcano's threats didn't seem to upset her at all. The mare hung her head over the stall and nuzzled his chest. He could see why Destante was so smitten with her.

Unfortunately, her fondness for the mare would keep Torag seeking her bed.

## CHAPTER 43

Later that morning, the sun was shining and a warm breeze flowed across the mountain where Destante walked with the lord of the manor. She was still exhausted from her exploits, but she could rest after she returned home again.

She spoke up. "Lord Torag, I thank you for your hospitality. You have been most generous. However, I'm sure you understand that we must take our leave. Time is pressing. I find I need to return home."

He sobered. "Surely you can stay longer. You've been ill and there are many plans to be made concerning Elis."

She nodded. "I have sent for all the Council to meet at my villa. We will discuss our plans then."

He smiled at her, took her hand, and leaned in close. "I will leave my wife here."

Again, Destante wondered about her sister's affairs. Torag was on a direct line between their own castle and

Elis. The day was almost there when the phoenix lord would discover she was not her sister. She had to be ready to stop him from giving his army to Elis. She didn't need Torag, but she DID need his army. She would put his amorous intentions into check when she could control what happened to his men.

As she mounted her gifted mare, she noted that Aniause was reticent, choosing to ride with the rear guard rather than up front with her. She nodded to herself, though it drove the pain of losing him deeper into her heart. She'd suspected the kiss the previous night had been a brash reaction to their nearness. Nothing more. Now, it seemed, he regretted their actions and was determined not to let it happen again.

So be it. The day was coming for him, too, of when he would have to make his final decision about their relationship, whether to protect the traditions of their ancestors, or change with the times. She hoped he would embrace new ways, but if not, she wasn't the first monarch of their kind to live forever without a mate. Head held high, she led the way toward her home.

When they had embarked on this journey, they'd gone in a diagonal manner to Balteus. Then straight across the east to Sharoth and Torag. Now, on their return trip, the third leg of the triangle traveled through two other lords' holdings. At both of these, they stopped dutifully, engaging in meals and small talk. Both men, Destante knew already as unremarkable in this upcoming battle. They would follow the strongest leader.

Once they arrived home, she would have liked to rest a couple days, but some of the Council were already there, requesting private audiences. Several of the other shapeshifter clan leaders from the south had also arrived: werewolves, bears, giant pythons and various birds.

Though the villa was large, sprawled across the mountain with 20 sleeping rooms, Destante couldn't walk the grounds without happening upon someone who wished to speak to her.

She had no inclination for subterfuge and whispered conspiracies. What needed to be discussed would be done so in the open, with all present. Instead, she threw herself into an inventory of her estate and belongings while waiting for the rest of the Lords to arrive.

Her two handmaids, who glared at each other with narrowed, jealous eyes, assisted her. Consuela stood near, crowding Destante each time directions were given, concentrating more on annoying Adelita than the actual words said. Adelita, in contrast, dashed away to do her mistress's bidding, even before hearing all that was said.

Aniause's affable presence would have made the task easier, but that was out of the question for now. She rubbed her temples and called Uzdal. "I need you to buffer me from these two."

He raised his eyebrows, but wisely kept his mouth shut. Instead, next time she had to give orders to the two girls, he leaned on his sword beside Destante. Something about the weapon sobered the handmaids, though not completely.

By the first day's end of inventory, Destante went to Aniause's examination room. At her rap, he opened the door with wide, surprised eyes. His gaze flit across her face and, before she could tell him what she needed, he said, "I see you have another headache. Come in. I'll fix you something."

While he stirred the compound, he glanced at her,

frowning. "I'm concerned about these headaches. Perhaps we'd better find out what's causing them."

"I know what's caused this one: two green-eyed girls trying to vie for my loyalty. That, and knowing I have more days ahead of me with them."

"Ah." He nodded in understanding. Finishing the compound, he handed it to her. "Drink it all."

She wasn't sure if the bitterness made her head worse. She swallowed it quickly and handed the vial back. "And the other headache was caused by Torag."

"Then the remedy is to avoid all three of them."

"As if it's that easy. Torag just arrived and is trying to insinuate himself into my bed already."

Aniause carefully put the vial away and chose his words. "I'm sorry, I can't help with that."

He turned to face her directly. "But, while you were on your errand to Elis's, I spoke to Torag. He all but admitted to destroying Delcinae."

Destante pressed her lips together and nodded. She'd surmised as much. But hearing that one of her own people had orchestrated it nearly broke her heart.

## CHAPTER 44

That evening, Aniause sat alone in his room in the dark. The moon shone through the window just enough that he could see to pour the pulque from the flask into his goblet.

Through the fog in his head, he slowly became aware someone had entered the room and was standing right beside him. He lifted his goblet to his lips, drained it back, and poured another. His fifth? Sixth? He lifted the drink to his lips again, but a soft, cool hand was placed on his arm, effectively stopping him.

A gentle voice quietly filled the room. His mother's voice. "Drink doesn't solve anything."

He jerked away from her touch. "What do you know? You're dead!"

The moonlight outlined the paleness of her face and her jet black eyes seemed to look straight into his inner being. Into the phoenix twisting in anguish there. She said, "Go to her."

"I can't." Emotion thickened his voice. He drank

the pulque in one big swallow and reached for the flask again. "She's the queen. I'm no royal blood."

His fingers fumbled on the corner of the flask, not quite grasping it. It tumbled to the floor, spilling the last of its contents. He lunged after it, violently tipping his chair and throwing himself down beside the empty flask. He lay still, looking up at his mother, drunken darkness crowding the edges of his vision. She'd died early in the war. He still missed her, even after all these years. "Maybe I should leave. I can't stand the thought of seeing her with someone else. I love her too much."

He pressed his head on the cool floor, letting the marble cool his cheek. He squinted his eyes and his mother's face slowly shifted into that of his friend, Pirien. Then Aniause passed out.

CHAPTER 45

Javier straightened in the darkness of King Noll's private bed chamber. Another dark shadow materialized on the other side of the bed: Miguel Angél.

It had taken them two full days of hard riding to reach Noll's castle grounds. They'd had no trouble avoiding the guards, entering through one of the many secret pathways hidden throughout the castle. But now they were here.

Miguel Angél let out a soft hiss. Javier followed his gaze.

The king wasn't alone.

A black-haired beauty lay sleeping softly beside Noll, her long woven hair coiled on the pillow beside her.

As if realizing she wasn't alone, her eyes fluttered open, focusing on Javier.

Before she could scream, he clamped his hand over her mouth. She gave a violent jerk, bumping against the king before she lay still, tears streaming down the side

of her face to the pillow below. He placed his finger
against his lips and the girl stifled her sobs, nodded, and
slid out of bed.

Noll stirred, but didn't wake.

Miguel Angél, a mask of vengeance on his face
and a serpentine spark in his eyes, moved in close to the
king and raised his knife.

CHAPTER 46

By the time the majority of the council of phoenix lords arrived, Destante was ready. They met in the dining hall, the only place large enough for such a gathering. This first meeting was closed to the other shapeshifters. She had business to deal to the phoenix lords.

She sat at the head of the table, listening. Besides herself, there was Baldric, Torag, Sharoth, twelve other lords, Aniause, Pirien, and her Army Chief, Uzdal. Two lords from the north, and one from the east, hadn't bothered to show to her summons.

Torag was speaking, his subterfuge obvious. "I believe Noll the only threat here. Elis is his whipping boy."

Pirien spoke up. "Whipping boy or not, he still could pose a threat."

Torag snorted. "Not on his own."

Baldric said, "I believe the Queen has some information concerning this."

They quieted and all turned to watch her, some with open contempt on their faces. She cleared her throat, and then said, "As long as we can force Elis to fight before their treaty is signed, I believe Noll will stay out of it. The dragon is Elis's goal, not necessarily Noll's. However, I've taken action to ensure Noll doesn't get involved. I've also sent for the various shifters who live south of us. Some are already here."

She turned to Balteus, Sharoth, and Torag. "How big are your armies combined?"

Lord Nalad from the northwest of Balteus interrupted, with amused disbelief on his face. "So that's it! You intend us to donate our armies to your cause?"

"I do. We are all in this together."

A general uproar exploded around the table. Baldric looked amused, while Aniause and Pirien had worried expressions on their faces.

"And leave us exposed to invasion? I won't do it." Torag stood. Destante's guards immediately stepped in front of the doors. He looked at her in astonishment. "Do you mean to keep us prisoner until we agree with you?"

"No, only until I've said everything I've intended to say. Then you may go. Sit, please."

He took one last look around the table and slowly sat.

Destante now stood and began to walk around the table. "With any new administration there are changes. For example, over the last three days, I personally have undertaken a complete inventory of the holdings of this palace and found not all the items on the books, nor the moneies, are actually here. I realize these items were sold or given for briberies. However, when the funds ended, my sister was killed. I, myself, was killed and

166

dismembered, but had the accident of rejoining. Now, it seems, we have been further betrayed by those who enjoyed those very same bribes. They intend to join with Elis."

Several of the lords nodded, some smiling. The sound in the room, however, was quiet as a death's hush.

She continued. "There is, of course, more than one person. There would have to be, in order to make such a fortune disappear so quickly. Most traitors will be jailed, and their families cast out of their homes. All their holdings will be taken as property of the court, which I'm sure most of it came from, anyway. Rest assured, when I confirm who the few remaining unknown traitors are, their fate shall join their friends."

She nodded at Uzdal and he stepped up behind Torag, lifting him from the seat and placed him in irons. One of the guards took custody and led him from the room.

Murmuring and nodding coursed the table, now. It seemed she was winning several of the lords to her side. Even those with contempt on their faces in the beginning had begun to soften.

Balteus spoke, a sly pitch to his voice. "And how do you intend to pay this army? Do you now have enough in your coffers? I'm not sure there's enough in the whole kingdom to pay them."

She stopped walking around the table and stared directly at him. "I'm sure there is."

The noise around the table stopped, and everyone stared at her. The wait grew heavy on the air, and a few began to fidget and look questioningly at each other. At last Baldric spoke. "Tell us, My Queen."

"Many of you tax excessively. Far beyond any measure of need. There's no need; you've been alive for centuries and are wealthy beyond belief. The monies my kin have spent on bribes were also on your behalf. Or do you forget what Elis and Noll can do? I want half."

The room exploded in anger. Her army chief, Uzdal, moved into a defensive stance beside her as several of the lords jumped to their feet. Balteus, as well as two others, stormed to the door, only to find the guards still blocking their way. Balteus whirled. "You can't do this. It's piracy! Release us at once!"

She stared directly into his eyes. "No."

He frantically sought around the room. "Lord Baldric! Brother. What do you say?"

From behind her, she heard the answer, filled with loathing. "You are no brother of mine. I support My Queen and have already sent for my tithe."

Relief flooded through her. With Baldric on her side, the others she wanted would follow. The rest didn't matter.

"What!?! You can't mean it! This is robbery!" Balteus stepped around Destante to meet Baldric face to face. She turned with him, keeping him in her sights.

"It is the only way we will be strong enough. I give my tithe." Baldric bowed to her. Behind him, five other lords also bowed.

"No! I'll not do it!" Balteus straightened himself.

Now she slammed her fist on the table and shouted, "Make no mistake, this is a time of fighting and battles like you've never seen! And I will do what's necessary in order that we have a chance at winning! If that means you will not support your kingdom in this time of crisis, then you are on the opposite side. I give you one last chance to offer your allegiance."

All the rest of the lords, but for Balteus and one form the North, Feldak, bowed. Balteus jutted out his jaw. "Then it shall be that we are at odds with each other. In time, others will join us."

"No, they won't. I don't have time to fight a civil war right now." She stepped out of the way, and Uzdal's men seized Feldak and Balteus, binding their arms tightly behind them.

She said, "You and your families are evicted from this kingdom, now and forever. Your holdings are now entirely property of this court. Even now, soldiers are being dispatched to collect what is now mine."

Feldak began to tremble. "Where do you intend to send us?"

Destante shook her head. "I don't care, but I sincerely doubt anyone will want you, except for perhaps Noll and Elis."

Balteus paled and Feldak fell to his knees, saying, "Forgive me, My Queen! I offer you my allegiance!"

"Men such as you cannot think on your own. You only follow the strongest. You follow a foolish man, and you pay his price. It is done."

As Uzdal's men led the two lords out of the room, Baldric spoke quietly to her. "You intentionally forced them to side against you."

"I did. In the time of battle, we don't need those of two minds."

Now she raised her voice to be heard. "I will need some men from your armies now, to help with the draft, and the gathering of tithes from all the lords. However, those of you on Elis's and Noll's borders, I want you to begin amassing men and place them at Lord Baldric's disposal. Lord Sharoth, I give you Lord Torag's men. Balteus's men as well."

Destante crossed to the windows and opened them. She turned back to the room and the guards that were at the door left, leaving the doors wide open. Servants brought new drink and food. "Gentleman Lords, please sit again. Invite your brethren shifters from the south to join us. Let us discuss the upcoming battle."

CHAPTER 47

The griffin, Elis, flew in the lower fringes of the afternoon clouds and volcano smoke, sending them into eddies and whirls with each flap of his giant wings. Griffins may not be high fliers, but they were the fiercest of all the shapeshifters. None could stand before them and they'd proven it by nearly driving the dragons into extinction. Now he, Elis, grand-nephew to the great Efar, who slew the dragon prince, Bartholemew, and started the war, had the honor of dispatching the last living dragon.

All because a man had come to him, telling of a secret among the phoenixes.

He was tired of waiting for the phoenix queen to decide what to do. She knew what he intended. She should have made her offer of peace by now. It had been five days since her visit to his castle. One glance at the quiet little man she'd pretended to be and he'd guessed it was her. Javier's presence had confirmed it. It had confused him when neither had said anything.

It was rude for a monarch to visit in disguise.

Insulting.

But, he had to admit that he'd deserved it after sending Cardenas and his son into her house under false pretense.

She was gutsy, that was for sure. Certainly not like her sister, who'd made liaisons through the bedroom. If he could tame a woman like that, what a prize she'd be on his arm.

The eagle part of him voiced a fierce, ear-piercing cry. The sound echoed back to him from the banks of clouds, amplifying until it was the only sound.

The time of waiting was done.

CHAPTER 48

In the second day of deliberations, Destante noted Javier quietly slip in the door of the great hall where she had sequestered herself and all those planning the upcoming battle.. He nodded, and sudden confidence filled her. Her enemy had been cut in half. And just in the nick of time.

Only moments before, Uzdal had been called away in a hurry. He returned, flinging open the doors of the great hall. Eddies of dust from the volcanic smoke swirled across the floor. "My Queen, King Elis is here."

Destante jerked her head up from where she was studying the map of her properties. She narrowed her gaze, waiting until the uproar of the council died away. Had Elis discovered Javier's mission already? She quietly asked, "Alone? Does he have his army waiting just across the border?"

"I don't think so. He landed at the gates, by himself." The Army Chief hesitated, then slowly, carefully said, "He's on the hacienda now."

She called to a servant. When he stood before her,

she said, "Prepare a room for the guest that is in my court right now; move someone if need be. Tell the cook to quickly place a feast on our table."

As he left, she looked around the room at the men gathered to plan the upcoming fight. "This may be a first step toward a treaty. We will not waste it. If you feel you cannot treat our guest as such, then you may choose not to attend the meal. At the end of this meeting, we may be enemies and at war, but for now, we are friends and civilized neighbors."

She sighed and turned to Baldric. "Now, you and I will greet our guest."

He silently fell in beside her, a heavy frown on his face.

When they arrived, Elis wasn't on the hacienda. Destante sat in her chair and said to Baldric, "Find King Elis, tell him he may see me at his pleasure. Then return to me, here."

Baldric bowed and left. Within a few minutes, he reentered the courtyard with Elis close behind. The griffin king was dressed in a simple robe, one of those kept at the front door of the villa for occasions when flying shifters visited, such as this one. Even still, with his height and his dark eyes, he was an imposing figure.

Destante stood and held out her hand. "Good evening, King Elis. It is my pleasure to have you visit."

He kissed her hand, and then said, "I have been remiss, Queen Destante. Congratulations on usurping the crown from this one." He cast a sly grin to Baldric.

Destante smiled. "Thank you. Though difficult at first, Lord Baldric and I have become united in our goals."

Elis raised his eyebrows at her warning. "I've come to speak of many matters that affect us both."

"Let's not speak on an empty stomach. I have

prepared a feast in honor of your visit. You will, of course, stay.”

“In truth, My Queen, I had not intended to do so.”

“There is always time to be civilized. We will speak of these matters as we eat.”

He hesitated, and then smiled and bowed. “Certainly, My Queen. It would be my privilege to dine with you.”

They walked into the dining hall, and Destante was pleased to note that most of her council had decided to attend. They cautiously shuffled to seats, furtively glancing at the visiting king. And, as always, the ground growled beneath their feet, reminding them of the volcanic threat.

Elis glanced from face to face, greeting some by name as he was seated, and Destante made note of those he knew. The griffin king didn’t act like a man who was on the brink of losing a battle. Rather, he behaved with the confidence of a visiting ally. Perhaps, then, he didn’t know about Noll. But the man was not to be trusted, either way.

As the servants brought the wine and the food, she leaned back in her chair and said to Elis, “I have seen you before. Up close, I mean.”

He nodded. “Yes, in my court. You were dressed as a man, with that rabscallion Javier.”

“Javier is my bodyguard. He argued quite hard to keep me from going to see you. But I meant earlier, when we were younger. In Spain. It was a ball your father hosted.”

He narrowed his eyes and stared off in an imaginary distance. After a moment, he shook his head. "I'm sorry, but I don't remember. If I had known you'd someday be queen, I'm sure I would have paid more attention."

She smiled, noting at the same time the absolute silence of her other guests as they listened to the conversation. "It isn't your fault. I'm sure if I knew I was going to be queen, I wouldn't have been so resistant to attending royal functions. The trouble with being a Phoenix is believing things will never change. In my mind, I shouldn't be on the throne, even still."

"Why didn't you announce yourself when you visited the other day?"

"I wanted to know you."

"And do you? Know me?"

"I believe I do. Tell me if I'm wrong. You believe in a strong rule, an iron fist. You've lived in peace next to a dragon for centuries, yet now that you know it, you suddenly decide he's a problem. Though, in truth, I think you suspected his presence all along. I believe he's an excuse. You intend to give my kingdom to your son, should you win, don't you? Or will you annex mine to yours and give Noll's to him? Yes, I think that's the way you intend it."

"I do indeed. I know you as well. No one knows how you survived Lord Baldric's attempt to kill you. Rest assured, your sister is NOT coming back. Javier is rumored to be your lover. Though I find that hard to believe, considering your love for another. I know you are building an army in secret. And doing it at an amazing rate. I commend you. But, it is still a trifling size, and certainly still very green."

"Javier? Really?" Destante glanced at Aniause in amusement, to find his face red as he suddenly concentrated on his food. Was he jealous? She turned her attention back to Elis. "Well, as long as the rumors keep the suitors away, who's to argue? You won't find me repeating my sister's performance as peacemaker."

"So what is to be done about this problem we

have?"

"You're not getting that dragon."

Elis stared at her a minute and then leaned back, laughing loud. As his laughter died away, he wiped his eyes. "I haven't laughed like that in a long while. It is too bad we're at odds. I would have liked your … friendship. There is no chance of treaty or alliance?"

"If I'd thought an alliance would have saved the dragon, I would have welcomed it. As Baldric did. But, I believe you would have betrayed him eventually and taken the dragon despite your assurances otherwise. As you intend to do with me, should we align. It is your nature."

"So we are enemies, then?"

"Friends may disagree, yet still not go to battle."

"Are you willing to go against the fiercest fighters of all the shapeshifters?"

She smiled. "Are you willing to go against a foe who keeps returning from the dead? Seems to me, I have the winning hand."

"You know my men won't be satisfied with just killing those of your kind. Even you will be tortured brutally."

Destante shook her head. "There's nothing you can do that I haven't endured before. I have been hung, decapitated, drowned, drawn and quartered. I've burnt in fire and acid, been poisoned, starved, and fed to animals. There isn't much more to the imagination."

Elis raised his eyebrows, then after a moment, slowly nodded. "Perhaps. I will think on our problem. And send message." He stood.

"One final thing." She motioned to Javier, who handed her a heavy cloth bag. From it, she withdrew Noll's head and tossed it at Elis's feet. "If you engage in battle with us, you'll be alone. My advice: forget the dragon.”

A myriad of emotions played across his face. He said tightly, “I commend your strategy. I will send my message tomorrow.” With that, he strode from the hall. Baldric followed at a distance.

When her phoenix lord returned, he spoke quietly, “I sent my guard to ensure Elis’s departure. He has already given his answer.”

She knew from the furrow on Baldric’s brow. She spoke to those present. “Now we prepare for battle.”

## CHAPTER 49

Aniause watched Destante through half-closed eyes. Just a short hour before, she'd received the enemy king's terse message. She'd called the lords back to the great hall, abandoning the feast. Now, she stood before her council, having delivered that message, waiting for the roar of outrage and disgust to die down.

The door in the front opened and Pirien slipped in, winding around the council members until he reached Aniause, who was seated in the back. Respectfully, the men nearby made space for the ancient priest to sit.

After a few moments of watching the arguments wage back and forth across the room, Pirien leaned in and whispered, "She's really come into her own, hasn't she?"

Aniause nodded, not taking his gaze off her. "She's a fine queen, but we knew she would be."

"Indeed."

Pirien seemed satisfied to watch the commotion a few more minutes, but then leaned in again. "A word of advice from an old man. There are all kinds of fools. There's the fool who has what he wants, but throws it away, and then there's the fool who refuses to fight for what is rightfully his."

He gestured toward Destante and continued whispering to Aniause. "You, my young friend, are both. Things change. The world changes. Her heart is rightfully yours and you threw it away."

Aniause turned to answer, to tell Pirien to mind his own business, but before he could speak, Destante held up her hand to silence those in the room. With a glare at the old man beside him, Aniause faced forward to hear what his queen would say.

When the room quieted, she began. "King Elis has reminded me that there are no fiercer creatures in the sky than griffins. We all know this is true. First hand. We've had many battles with them over the course of the greater war.

"But, his words also remind me that," she held up one finger, "they aren't so tough on the ground. In fact, they're quite easily beaten there. Even more so if they refuse to shift into the creature. They put too much faith in their creature's strength."

A second finger joined the first. "They cannot fly as high as we do. They're only half eagle. In fact, there are no shifters of any kind who can reach our heights, except the hawk, a full eagle, and of course the dragon. Therefore, it seems to me we should wait in the clouds, or the cold fringes between light and dark, and then force them to the ground."

She swept her hand flat, palm up, encompassing the men standing and sitting around the room. "Let us pursue ideas along this vein of thought for a few moments." She smiled.

The room was still while the men considered her

words, then a slow murmur began. Someone Aniause could not see, nor recognize by voice, spoke up from the far rear corner of the room. "The volcano complicates things. Its threats are hard to ignore. The last time Colima rumbled, nothing happened; the smoke and tremors faded away. Will we be so lucky a second time? Perhaps we should do as the natives of this land have and find refuge elsewhere."

Destante shook her head. "The only place we could go is south. We're not familiar with that terrain. Elis will certainly not wait for us to return. He will follow us and prompt the battle there. We have a small chance of winning here, but there winning would fall completely to those shifters. It is not their battle. It is ours."

The room fell into silence again.

Finally, Baldric spoke. "There is the problem of forcing a griffin in flight to go where we choose, My Lady. We need them low so our arrows can help us. They will know that."

Aniause stood. "My Queen, I believe I may be able to help with that."

All eyes turned toward him. The ground trembled Colima's promise.

"While studying medicine in the Orient, I encountered a powder that was being used as air decorations. It was lit and sent up into the air, where it exploded, shooting sparks in all directions. They called it 'fireworks'."

Destante slowly nodded. "We could frighten them with it. That would certainly help." She made as if to turn away.

Hurriedly, he added, "Additionally, My Queen, some small groups attached this powder to their arrows to give them a greater lift."

Her face lit and her eyes seemed to spark. Beside

her, both Javier and Uzdal broke into grins.

She said, "Are you able to procure this powder for us? Will we get it in time?"

Aniause cleared his throat. "My Queen, I have the recipe."

CHAPTER 50

Destante, Aniause, Javier, Baldric, and Uzdal sat on their horses, looking down from a hilltop, watching Elis's army approach the tree lined river that began Destante's kingdom. Colima thundered the ground in near constant tremors and belched thick black smoke, adding to the sobriety of the day, darkening the skies, the earth, and everyone who moved within it. It was so dark, the army looked like a black moving sea, inching up into a green-black sand with the tide.

Unbidden, her mind slipped back to one battle after another. So many battles. So many seas of men, most dead now. She cleared her throat. "That's a lot of soldiers."

Baldric nodded. "He has thousands."

"We'll parry it down to size. Have you seen Elis yet?"

"No. But he's there. He always fights in disguise as one of his men until he takes to the skies."

She snorted. "As if we don't know he's there, or

that there are already griffins in the skies."

Turning to Aniause, she asked, "Do you have everything ready? You added the fireworks to all the arrows?"

He nodded. "I do. I think you'll be pleased. Not only will the arrows go further, but will explode in the sky or upon impact."

Baldric spoke up again. "Forgive me for saying so, My Queen. But I dislike this sneaky manner of fighting you have ordered, like we're thieves. It seems dishonorable to go to battle climbing in trees, hiding in holes in the ground, and laying traps. I feel that if we cannot win as shifters or men, then we shouldn't win. We have archers, shifters, and fliers. It should be enough."

"I understand. I don't care for it much either, but in the end, it's who is the smartest that wins. Never who is the strongest. Though strength certainly doesn't hurt. But, if that's the way you feel, Lord Baldric, then you should join Elis's soldiers and die with them."

"I meant no mutiny." His voice was quiet. Contrite. They were silent a short while before he added, "Wouldn't it bother you if I went over to him? I know your tricks."

"Do you, Lord Baldric? All of them?"

He barked a short laugh. "Your words make me think I don't."

She said, "Don't worry. You'll get your chance to fight like a man. But, we want to force them to bring the fight right where WE want it. Then you may have your man-to-man battle."

"You really believe this one battle will finish this war?"

She nodded. "That is my hope."

Below, the army had spread wide as they entered

the trees. Destante nodded and Baldric's archer let loose with a flaming arrow. A storm of Aniause's special arrows landed on one side of the advancing men. Explosions ripped through the air with dirt and debris. The men fell back, muddying their ranks. Some fell to the ground, apparently dead. The horses reared in terror.

Another volley of arrows, and more explosions ripped on the other flank. More fell to the ground. The army below scattered out of the trees.

Destante's gifted black mare danced a jig at the commotion. Javier's horse merely stood, trembling, while Baldric's was rearing and plunging, fighting to bolt.

Aniause moved his horse in close, pressing against her, his own horse steady. The mare quieted beneath her. She said, "Very nice. Perhaps Elis will listen to the message we send."

They watched as the generals below regained control of their men. Riders from the middle of the army rushed forward.

Destante pointed. "There. Did you see where they came from?"

Javier pointed. "Elis. He wears the single red plume in his helmet."

It took her half a second to find him. He was in the thick of the forefront of his army, gesturing to the men around him. Two of those men were the same who'd entered her home: Cardenas and Elis's own son. Now that she saw him, she understood the layout of his army. His front men were expendable. It was the flanks they had to worry about. They'd done well with the fireworks arrows. Those best warriors were the ones getting hit.

The plumed figure in the crowd below dismounted

his horse and began pulling off his armor.

Destante nodded, more to herself than anyone else. "He's shifting to griffin."

Baldric scanned the sky above them. "Doubtless others of his kind are already waiting in the clouds to ambush us."

She laughed loudly at him. "What, Dear Cousin, is the difference between that kind of ambush and the one where we wait in trees and holes in the ground? Besides the location, of course."

He shrugged, then his gaze slid to the side, and he jutted his jaw to the line of trees directly to their right. "My Queen, the priest approaches."

Frowning, she turned to glare at Pirien as he wove his mount through the grove of mesquite trees. When he reached their group, she said, "You shouldn't be here."

Instead of answering, the old man dismounted. He stretched his back, hands on hips, his ancient bones popping and snapping. Then, he turned to her and softly said, "This is precisely where I should be. You know it as well as I."

With that, he began to grow. His richly tapestried robes split at the seams and sloughed to the ground. Scales formed to cover every inch of his skin, deepening to forest green and gold. Bat-like wings sprouted from his back. His face elongated and dagger-like teeth snicked into place. His arms stretched and thickened, sprouting scimitar claws.

He reached the size of his horse, and still he grew. Dragons weren't like other shifters, who had a finite size. Instead, dragons continued growing until they died.

Aniause nudged Destante and glanced pointedly at Javier.

Her bodyguard sat stonily on his mount, but his

mouth was wide open. His face was pale and his eyes were nearly popping out of his head. His horse, having been raised with the others around the scents of dragon and phoenix, showed little concern.

Pirien reached the size of the trees around them, and his growth began to slow. He lowered his head, spread his mighty wings and bellowed a roar straight from the prehistoric era when monsters roamed the earth. It rang across the mountain range, echoing and filling the spaces in the valley below, stopping everyone to stare.

A thrill ran up Destante's spine and she gave Aniause a wolfish grin.

## CHAPTER 51

Destante swung to the ground from the back of her little brown mare, spouting orders and shifting at the same time, her clothes puffing in a cloud as they split from the immediate change. She ignored the searing pain of a quick change, and her final words sounded hollow, as if spoken into a bucket, coming out of her half-formed beak. "...Baldric on his right. Aniause and I will fly on his left flank. Two people with him at all times. We'll give them the dragon, all right. Right down the middle of their forces."

Pirien gave a rumble deep in his long, long throat.

Uzdal appeared out of nowhere with the saddle pack from Pirien's horse. The army general tossed it high. Within would be the brimstone the dragon needed to breathe fire.

The dragon's serpentine neck whipped through the air and he caught the pack neatly in his jaws. One swallow and it was gone. Then he turned his cool green gaze on Destante. It felt as if she were pulled into that

188

hypnotic stare. Down into a deep abyss. The dragon blinked. He thrust with his powerful hind legs and flapped mightily with his monstrous wings.

Destante, now completely phoenix, hissed urgently at Aniause and Baldric, then launched after the dragon. They circled above the foray on the ground, until all four of them were in formation.

Reaching deep inside her for that well of life, that spark that begged for freedom, Destante burst into flames. Like before, her senses heightened and the hunger for battle overtook her. The fire was so hot upon her, Aniause and Baldric both veered from their places beside her to fly a distance off her wing.

In one hard, fast dive, three phoenixes and one dragon rocketed toward the grounded troops, skimming above them, igniting shields, clothing, hair, grass, shrubs, trees, and flesh. The stench filled her senses, stoking the fire that consumed her. She gave a piercing war cry. It was followed closely by the dragon's roar.

Take her dragon, would they? Attempt a battle on her? They were learning how in error they'd been.

She noted that Elis, nor his son, nor his elite guard were not among the dead and dying. They had completed their shift to griffin and were probably up in the skies already.

The four of them circled for another pass. From a distance, arrows flew at them, but none could penetrate the dragon hide, nor her flames. Baldric and Aniause withdrew out of range to avoid being hit. Below, Javier and Uzdal brought the army right behind the initial attack and their swords were meting out hell on Elis's forward troops.

Destante and Pirien stayed high enough to not injure their own soldiers, then swooped low on the enemy behind, those waiting to engage. The dragon again belched fire in long plumes ahead of them, while Destante flew close in the midst of the frightened men. Those men that weren't burnt took refuge in the trees, where other shapeshifters hid.

Between the trunks of the trees, Destante saw men's bodies clashing against hard animal muscle, swords against claw and tooth. A group of werewolves drove a small cluster of Elis's men into the clearing, backing them into a cluster of the phoenixes' land soldiers. It seemed the forces on the ground were in good hands.

She thrust her long, plumed tail down and worked her wings to carry her to the heights where her brethren waited. The heavy gusts of air working beneath Pirien's giant wings buffeted her from behind.

All around her were the grunts and cries as Phoenix warred against Griffin. Beside them were other avian shifters: Hawks, Eagles, Crows, Sparrows, and a few exotics Destante couldn't name.

A desperate scream came from a gutted phoenix, one of the lords from the north of her region. He plummeted past her toward the earth, entrails trailing. He would be reborn.

Uzdal had men watching to rescue these casualties and move them to a secure location where they could regenerate later. This wasn't his first battle. Already he was dispatching someone to meet the phoenix where it landed.

Nor was it the first battle for the phoenixes. They'd been battling to keep the dragon safe for generations, ever since the war began over 1000 years ago. They all knew what to do.

As she rose through the clouds, they swirled around her, dissipating and hissing in reaction to her flames. The dispersed moisture condensed on the feathers of Baldric and Aniause so they looked bedraggled and wet. Aniause continuously shook his head to rid his eyes from the water. Volcanic smoke turned their feathers dark, matting them together into a heavy weave.

The sounds of battle increased, ebbing and flowing past the four of them while they climbed.

They broke out of the remnants of the uppermost clouds. Up there, there were only phoenixes, the dragon, and the sharp-eyed eagle and hawk shifters. The highest fliers. Heavy, all. Their sole job was to dive from above at the griffins, forcing them within range of the arrows. So it had always been since the beginning of the war, 1000 years ago. So it would be until the war was over.

The only change being the arrows that now flew higher, thanks to Aniause's spark-producing modifications.

Destante spotted a griffin with a crow in its clutches. She dove toward it, her flames crackling. The griffin either saw or heard her and suddenly flipped over, exposing its talons and the crow to her burning heat.

She pulled up and hesitated. Then she saw how deeply the griffin's talons gripped the crow's body, deep enough to have pierced the small bird's internal organs. Even if it got loose, it wouldn't live. The crow confirmed her fears with a weak struggle. Then its head lolled to the side, the life spark dying out of its eyes.

Fury erupted within Destante and she plummeted after the griffin, her flames burning white hot and roaring.

Too late, the griffin saw her, its eyes wide open in surprise. It had no time to react.

Its feathers smoked, then singed, and finally burst

into flames as she landed on the crow, hooking her talons deep through it into the burning griffin below. The momentum of her dive sent them downward at an incredible rate and the arrows that flecked the back of the griffin hadn't yet expended all Aniause's firework powder.

The griffin exploded.

The force of it sent Destante tumbling through the sky, frantically trying to right herself.

CHAPTER 52

Aniause's heart stalled as Destante tumbled through the air. Her wings flapped fiercely, seeking purchase in the wisps of clouds. Her beak was wide open and it seemed she had no grasp of up or down. It was entirely possible her ears had been damaged in the blast from the griffin.

It was in that exact moment, he suddenly understood what Pirien had been trying to tell him. It was something he'd always known, yet had somehow forgotten its implications. Destante was his one and only. His past and future. Phoenixes mated for all their lives. Because he and Destante were mated before she became queen, they were mated still. His current stupidity not withstanding. The world would adjust to allow them together. It was a changing world, after all.

Her flames extinguished and she plummeted toward the warring shifters on the ground below.

Aniause tucked his wings against his body and raced after her. He couldn't lose her now, even though she'd regenerate. He'd seen her die too many times, leaving too many scars on his heart. For a while, his scars had hidden the truth, but no more. He couldn't bear to see her die again. Not with his stupidity still between them. But first, he had to save her.

She spied him, and the look in her eyes was pure desperation.

The wind was heavy on him.

Shifters clashed all around them.

The volcano's growl drowned out all sound.

The ground loomed.

And then he was close enough. He grabbed her in his talons, fighting gravity, working his wings to slow their descent.

From above came Baldric's warning cry, quickly followed by Pirien's bellow of pain.

Three griffins had taken excuse of Aniause's and Destante's absence and had attacked the dragon. One had Pirien's long, sinewy neck trapped in its beak, while it clung to his belly like an upside down horseman. The second also clung to the top of Pirien's neck, working to slide its talons between the scales. The third flew at the dragon's eyes, seeking to peck and tear. It was this last that Baldric attacked.

Deep within Aniause, his nerves zinged, moving right into sharp pinpricks of pain. His head swam, and all sound, except that of the volcano, ceased. Natural birds swarmed into dark, panicked clouds near the ground in a high-speed escape.

The phoenix below him struggled to free herself. He let go.

Below them, the earth groaned.

All was quiet for half a minute. A pinprick of reddish-orange lit the tip of Colima's dome. The volcano thundered and, in a blinding flash, it flung molten lava and rock into the clouds, ash, and smoke.

A split second later, a shockwave hit. It hurtled Aniause and Destont through the air, fluttering helplessly and seeking purchase in the gusts of foul-smelling wind that blew from the volcano.

Aniause righted, checking to see that Destante had also leveled out and was racing toward the ground troops closest to the exploding volcano, as were the majority of her phoenix lords. He tore after his phoenix queen, straight into the densest of the outpouring smoke, dodging pelting rock and burning embers that spewed out of Colima, one eye always on the onslaught. Pinpricks of pain burned through his feathers and sharpened on his skin into lances from molten lava splatters.

A series of gargantuan boulders plummeted toward them. He followed Destante into a tight weave around the first few easily enough, heat rolling off waves from them. But the next three were closer together.

Ash and smoke were thick here, rolling down the side of the volcano like waves in the ocean. Through the haze, Aniause saw movement. For a second, he thought his eyes were playing tricks on him, labeling smoke swirls as living being, but then he saw the movement as consistent in its pattern. It WAS a person.

He glanced at Destante, but she veered toward another group of soldiers. The quickest way to any point was a direct line. Aniause ducked his head, streamlined his body, flapped his wings with every ounce of strength he had, and flew directly in the path of the oncoming boulders.

Smaller rocks, like missiles, pelted him from above and heat from the boulders bore down on him. The sharp pinpricks of blisters peppered his back and he ducked lower, skimming a couple feet off the earth.

He was close enough now, he could see the terrified soldier clearly: one of the griffin's. Aniause ground his beak together. A life was a life. He didn't slow. In passing, he snagged the man's shoulder with his talons, piercing through the tunic and chainmail, grasping the skin and bone below, and jerking the soldier off his feet. The man screamed in pain, but clothing tore and chainmail sometimes came apart.

Already, Aniause felt the weight of the rocks on his feathers. He swooped lower, brushing the ground with his belly, dragging the soldier behind him.

Then they breached the other side and the boulders crashed into the ground with a mind-jarring thunder. Aniause glanced behind him, noting a few missing tail feathers sticking out from beneath the rock and burning.

He raised into the air and took the soldier to safety. Several of the phoenix lords also had soldiers in their grips and were carrying them to safety, Destante among them.

There were no griffins assisting their own troops to safety.

CHAPTER 53

Destante dropped, none too easily, Elis's foot soldier with the others that had been carried to safety. She was pleased to see Aniause among many of her phoenix lords. He'd worried her when she lost him in the smoke and ash. She was going to change the laws after the battle, and she didn't care that it would appear self-serving. She couldn't be queen, couldn't do the job without him. And being unspoken mates wasn't enough anymore, not with everything they'd been through together. She intended to declare their bond for all the phoenix world to see. It would be official and written in the record books.

Satisfied the evacuation was well underway and with one last glance at her true love, she shot upward, flames trailing in her wake, searching for Pirien. The smoke was thick, nearly choking her, so she was almost on top of the scene before she knew it. The shock wave had apparently knocked the griffins loose from the dragon, but they were seeking purchase again. She saw now that one of them was Elis's son.

Pirien and Baldric were, so far, keeping them at bay, turning in circles to face the oncoming beaks and claws. Plumes of flames spouted from the dragon, while the phoenix lord faced down the griffins behind.

Destante came into the center of the group from below just as the griffin prince attacked Baldric, allowing another to reclaim the choke hold on Pirien's throat.

Destante came in close to the dragon's belly, trusting his scales hadn't been wedged apart and would protect him from her flames. The griffin, however, had no scales. It held on as long as it could, but the moment its feathers began to smoke, it let go of its prize and fell away to find something to sooth its blistered skin. A boulder from the volcano crashed against the griffin and drove it into the ground.

Baldric's battle with Elis's son had pulled out of range when Destante arrived, so the moment Pirien's neck was free from the griffin's crushing grip, the dragon twisted his head and shot a stream of flames at the remaining griffin. It screamed and burst into flame, dropping from the sky, like burning coal from a shovel.

Fairly sure none of those griffins had been Elis, Destante searched for the griffin king while Baldric continued his fight with the Elis's son. She found the king locked in battle with two of her phoenix lords, his lion claws and eagle talons and beak raking across tender bird flesh every time they came near.

Unease filled her. This all looked too familiar: the king out in the open, low hanging clouds of ash, scarcely any other griffins around. She ran through the memories of other battles and just as she settled on one, a squadron of griffins broke out of the lowest sooty clouds above her, driving straight at her in single file.

It was an old tactic: get rid of the fire-bearer so they had better odds with the dragon. The griffins each would burn as they closed on her heat, but they'd use the one in front as a buffer until it was gone. Eventually, they'd get all the way to her and be able to gut her, sending her crashing to the earth below, where their soldiers waited to distance her head from her body to keep her from regenerating.

It was wasteful, but effective. Many in her line had fallen this way. Her own father had. Then it hit her: that was why the griffins had sacrificed their soldiers; they'd given up everything for one final push to kill the last dragon and finish the war.

Destante eyed Elis. She could turn and attack him instead, as her father had attacked his father. But, griffins were faster and, though Elis's father had perished from the flames, so had her father from the griffins behind him.

She turned instead to face the squadron. So be it.

This had also been tried before. It also had failed. But she was the youngest phoenix in history to sit the throne; her youth might give her the edge.

Stoking her flames to white hot again, she drove right toward the line of griffins.

They tightened their line formation. They'd seen this before. They knew how it would end.

Destante reached deep inside, deep into where the phoenix lived, pulling on the fire that flickered there. She already felt herself burning even hotter than she'd ever thought possible. Still, she pulled on the fire. It was the same spark that had burned in every one of her ancestors. Soft memories of battles sifted around her. And still she pulled on the fire until those memories became one with the fire and consumed her from the inside out.

Long before the first in the line of griffins reached her, it caught fire. And the second. Then the third. The fourth. And on to the fifth. By the time she reached the head of the line, there was only black ash. By the middle of the line, the griffins were all burning to crumbles.

She circled out of the black cloud and checked on Elis's position.

He was deep in battle with the same two phoenix lords, but no less than five other bird shifters had joined in. Blood soiled his lion fur and eagle feathers, and he was nearly blinded by a gash across his face. His son was writhing on the ground far below; he was no phoenix, it would take a long time for him to heal.

The battle was nearly over. Most of Elis's griffins were defeated. His ground troops certainly were.

Pirien …

Pirien was nowhere to be seen. Neither were Aniause nor Baldric.

Something had happened while she'd been distracted.

She searched the ground, flying in ever widening circles. Her worst fears were confirmed when she spied Baldric alone, vigilantly circling over a tight cluster of mesquite, spruce, and buckeye trees well away from the damage of the volcano. A pair of horses were tied near the edge.

Dread nearly choking her, she swooped to the ground and was met by Uzdal with a robe. Shifting to human, she strode into the woods, tying the robe in place. Pirien was seated on a half-rotted, white log, his face masked in the shadows. Aniause stood nearby. Javier had his sword protectively in hand.

Destante settled beside Pirien.

He shook his head at her. "I'm tired. I just can't

keep this up."

"What do you mean?"

Aniause broke in, his eyes wide open. "It was you, wasn't it? You're the one who told Elis you were in our midst."

Pirien gave a weak smile. "It was. I will tell you my final secret. I'm not the last dragon. It has been my honor to buy time for the rest of my people to relocate and hide. It's now time for me to join them. This war has been going on for over a thousand years. It's time for the killing to stop before there are no shifters left. I could think of no way to keep the griffins from searching for me, other than to fake my death."

Destante nodded. He was right. She felt it within her. "What do you want me to do?"

"Tell them I've died from my injuries." He stretched his neck. "Actually, I think I nearly did."

"Elis will want to see for himself."

He gestured to Aniause. "Our young doctor can make me look dead. And dragons can hold their breath for a very long time."

She stood. "I'll get Elis."

CHAPTER 54

Destante walked out of the wooded cluster, stepping between sharp twigs and knotted clusters of leaves with her bare feet. Spruce needles carpeted the ground and lifted their heady scent wherever she walked. Her heart was breaking. Just when it looked like she and Aniause would be reunited again after the battle. Then this. Pirien was leaving them.

She knew her heart and what she wanted, and she knew her duty as queen. But, she also knew her vow to always protect the dragon, no matter what the consequence. It was a sacred calling that had been drilled into her since she was a child. ALL else was sacrifice to the dragon's safety. She couldn't ignore it. She had to leave with Pirien.

No amount of changing the laws would bring her and Aniause back together now. If he didn't want to be with her, she'd live her life alone. Deep-seated sorrow filled her.  She shed her robe and shifted into her phoenix, ignoring the crackle of pain that lanced through her bones. Fully flamed, she rose into the sky, the heat inside her stronger than the heat from the obscured Mexican summer sun, hotter than the volcano that continued to spew rocks and lava in defiance of the battle that surrounded it.

The griffins hadn't rescued their own men. Not a one. What kind of leader sacrificed all his men? How could he hold their loyalty except through fear? It said much about the predatory bird shifter. Her own phoenix lords had taken pity on Elis's ground-bound men and had flown many to safety. Many had pled their allegiance to her immediately. Still, the casualties on that side had been great.

She approached the griffin king. Those phoenix lords surrounding him, as well as a hawk and a few other birds, fell away from her heat, yet maintained a loose circle.

Fierce-eyed, the griffin whirled around and around, not having seen her approach, his sides heavy with exertion, nearly blinded by blood. More blood poured from deep gashes along his skin. Feathers were missing. It was clear he was losing the battle. Finally, he saw her, stopped dead and stared at her. He listed slowly toward his badly damaged right wing.

She extinguished her flames and turned toward the ground. At first, she heard nothing, then finally came the sound of lopsided griffin wings slowly beating the air behind her.

They landed side-by-side next to the grove of trees and took the robes Uzdal offered. She said to Elis, "The dragon is dying."

"Dying?" He narrowed his eyes. "He wasn't injured that badly."

"Perhaps not externally, but his breathing has been labored of late, and I think flying in the volcano ash may have finished him. Your men also helped by strangling him, I'm sure." She led the way through the white trunks to where Pirien, as dragon, lay stretched on his side. He was still as stone and looked dead, but if Elis were to believe it, then she, Aniause, and Javier would have to sell it.

She rushed forward, forcing fear and worry into her voice. "Am I too late? Has he gone?"

Aniause nodded and turned away, not even acknowledging Elis's presence. The physician's face was contorted into a dark mask of anguish. Destante thought she even saw tears.

She dropped to her knees beside the dragon's massive head, running her hands along his cheek. She leaned over, kissed his face, and whispered, "Goodbye, my friend."

Standing, she faced Elis and motioned to Pirien. "The last dragon is dead. Are you happy now? Does that satisfy you?" The bitterness that filled her voice was genuine. Pirien's death could have been real.

The griffin king stared at the dragon's still form in silence. He walked close to the dragon and placed his hand on the great creature's ribs. When there was no tremor of breath felt, he let his hand drop to his side.

Javier angrily strode into the grove and to Pirien's enormous head. He jerked his long sword out of its scabbard, and held it in readiness over the dragon's neck. He glared at Elis and his voice was filled with sarcasm. "Do you require a trophy, Sire?"

It wasn't lost on Elis. Fury lit across his features and he opened his mouth to speak. Then, apparently thinking better of it, he frowned and shook his head. Stared at the giant body of his fallen enemy again.

Destante cleared her throat. "The last dragon is dead; this ancient war is over. I suggest you gather your troops and get off my land while you can. As soon as my people find out what happened, they'll seek retribution."

Elis startled and looked at her with confusion.

"I won't be able to control them," she said softly.

He gave an abrupt nod and, after one last glance at the dragon's prone form, strode out of the grove, shedding his robe and shifting to griffin at the same time.

Destante glanced back at Pirien. How long could a dragon hold its breath? If he even took a small inhale now, Elis's keen lion and eagle senses would hear it, even from the heights. She followed the griffin king, scuffing her toes on the ground, crushing leaves and snapping sticks.

Baldric approached the still rising Elis to attack, but when it became clear the griffin wouldn't engage, he circled and landed beside Destante. Without waiting for him to shift, she said, "Collect our men. The war is over."

Even as she turned to Uzdal, the air rippled around her from Baldric's take off. "Uzdal, round up the shifters on the ground. Thank them and send them home. Tell no one of the dragon's death. We don't need to start a new war right now. They'll find out soon enough."

He bowed and left. Destante returned to Aniause and Javier. The men were grim, watching her approach. It was dangerous business, tricking a griffin king. Tricking all the shapeshifter world. They'd have to be perfect in every detail and allow no one to ever know the truth.

Her bodyguard opened his mouth to speak, but she shook her head, motioning him to silence. The griffin might still be within hearing distance, or there might be a spy left behind. She put as much sorrow into her words as she could. "Javier, you're to stay here to guard the dragon's body. Help Aniause prepare it for a ceremonial burning."

She'd leave it to the two of them to find something big enough to burn in Pirien's place. They would also make sure he returned home safely when he finally awoke again. He'd have to hide in his quarters until they could get him to his people. No one could know Pirien was still alive.

CHAPTER 55

It was the evening of the fourth day since the war ended. Aniause was in his lab, preparing the next day's ointments and pain killers. He'd taken some time to clean the piles of papers and musty books that usually covered his tables. The vials, bottles and packets were freshly filled and stacked neatly away. He'd even had a maid come in, under his watchful eye, to take a cloth to the dust that usually coated every corner of his laboratory and to scrub the floor.

Between that, and doctoring the various injuries earned in the fight, he'd been busy. Very busy. But things were slowing down now. Most cuts and burns were well on the way toward being mended. All that remained to be treated were the deep lacerations and redressing the worst of the burns with fish skin.

To assist with the injured, Aniause had sent for a physician from the village and had been coaching him in the various treatments used on the phoenix kind. His only regret, thus far, was that he'd had no time to speak with Destante. Nor had he seen her since that day in the grove. He wasn't the only busy person, it seemed.

Pirien had been scarce, too, since returning the first night, traveling on a tram as a body. Stiff and sore, he'd climbed onto Aniause's table without complaint. Other than a few severe bruises and puncture wounds around his neck, the ancient priest had fared the battle well. It had taken twelve cows to take the place of the dragon on the funeral pyre. They'd been skinned and dismembered, smuggled that first night by Javier and a couple of Baldric's most loyal men, and carefully arranged in a dragonish shape. They were burning still, days later, tended hourly so that no one would see the remains that were obvious cow parts.

He stacked the most recent packets of remedies for his rounds to the injured, carried them to the door, and stalled, face-to-face with the phoenix queen.

They stared at each other.

His mouth dried, and his heart thudded heavily against his ribs. He was speechless. After all these centuries, she still had the same affect on him.

Aniause said the first thing he could drag to mind. "Some of the other shifters have discovered the dragon's death, believing it to be true. They're hunting down Elis's men. I don't think they'll quit any time soon."

She nodded, picked up a jar, and inspected it. "They want vengeance. And to everyone's purposes, it *is* true."

"I don't blame them."

"If it were true."

"Yes." He was such an oaf. Why couldn't he just tell her the real thing that was on his mind? It was now or never. He slowly walked to her and took her hands. "I'm sorry. I shouldn't have said we couldn't be together."

"Yes. You were quite the idiot." Anger flashed in her eyes. Then her gaze softened, moistened. She smiled, but then sadly shook her head. "It doesn't matter anymore –"

"But, I can't –"

She held up a hand, forestalling his words. She said, "Pirien is ready to join his brethren. I'm going with him."

"What? Where?"

She shook her head. "I can't tell you. It's better that no one knows. They're all supposed to be dead, remember?"

Shock held him silent a moment. He'd finally done it. He'd driven her away. He'd said all those foolish things about not being together, and she'd decided she'd had enough. He found his voice, it was loud. Strident. "You're Queen. You can't just leave."

"Actually, I can. Baldric has proven he's more than capable of handling the throne, now that there's no threat of war. I even believe we'll both have flames, like in earlier generations, when there were more phoenixes in the skies. People will simply assume he did away with me to take the throne, like he tried before."

Aniause shook his head violently and opened his mouth to speak, but she held up her hand again to stay him, saying, "When I was young, I made a sacred vow to protect the dragon with my life. I must go."

"Destante, I —"

She turned away. "There's nothing you can say or do to change the facts. I must go."

Then she was gone.

Aniause stared at the empty place where she'd stood. What now?

After a moment, he gave himself a mental shake and turned back to his ointments and vials. He needed time to figure everything out. Still, his mind tumbled over the conversation. She was leaving. And there wasn't anything he could do about it. He picked up his stack of packets again, to begin his rounds, but he couldn't make himself walk out the door. He kept seeing her face, the love and forgiveness in her eyes. Kept hearing her final words.

Then, like a spark that went off, like one of his firework arrows that exploded in the sky, it came to him: she hadn't said goodbye.

She wanted him to decide on his own what he would do, without pressure from her. If he went with them, it was because he wanted to be with her, no matter what the difficulties. Given everything he'd put them through, he certainly understood her reasoning.

He couldn't live without her. He knew this. All he wanted was to be with her, kingdoms, dragons, and traditions be damned.

Energy coursing through him, he called a passing aide and handed over the prepared medicines. "Please deliver these to the injured. They should last a few days. There's a physician in the village. Tell him I've left. He'll know what to do."

Rushing to the courtyard, he spied Javier. But the bodyguard had already seen him and was pointing out to sea. The moon was partially obscured, but it was bright enough he could still see two specks floating over choppy water, headed east.

In a split second, Aniause shifted to phoenix, barely feeling the deep wells of pain that raced through his bones, clothes exploding in a giant cloud. He took two running strides, then launched over the rolling ocean below, flying as hard as his wings could push him. The stink of the volcanic ash that held the land in its grip loosened out there, over the water, and he pulled in the first deep breaths of fresh clean air that he'd taken in days.

In no time, he caught up with the pair, Destante on the left and Pirien on the right. They were flying slow, letting the ocean breezes lift them. As if waiting....

The old dragon kept his attention steadfastly on the horizon, but Destante turned and locked her gaze on Aniause. There seemed to be a glint of humor in her eyes. She gave a soft trill of pleasure that drove straight to his heart. Aniause moved in close to Destante, brushing her wingtips with his.

In that moment, he felt all the love they'd shared through the centuries past, and all they would share in the future. Mates forever.

<u>THE END</u>